KU-411-654

COLETTE

Colette, the creator of Claudine, Cheri and Gigi,
and one of France's outstanding writers, had
a long, varied and active life. She was born in
Burgundy on 1873 into a home overflowing with
dogs, cats and children, and educated at the local
village school. At the age of twenty she moved
to Paris with her first husband, the notorious
writer and critic Henry Gauthiers-Viller (Willy).
By locking her in her room, Willy forced Colette
to write her first novels (the *Claudine* sequence),
which he published under his name. They were
an instant success. Colette left Willy in 1906
and worked in music halls as an actor and
dancer. She had a love affair with Napoleon's
niece, married twice more, and had a baby at 40
and at 47. Her writing, which included novels,
portraits, essays and a large body of autobio-
graphical prose, was admired by Proust and
Gide. She was the first woman President of the
Académie Goncourt, and when she died, aged
81, she was given a state funeral and buried in
Père Lachaise Cemetery in Paris.

ALSO BY COLETTE

Fiction

Claudine at School
Claudine in Paris
Claudine and Annie
Gigi
The Cat
Chéri
The Last of Chéri
Chance Acquaintances
Julie de Carneilhan
The Ripening Seed
The Vagabond
Break of Day
The Innocent Libertine
Mitsou
The Other One
The Shackle

Non-fiction

My Apprenticeships and Music-Hall Sidelights
The Blue Lantern
My Mother's House and Sido
The Pure and the Impure

COLETTE

Claudine Married

TRANSLATED FROM THE FRENCH BY
Antonia White

VINTAGE

12

Vintage
20 Vauxhall Bridge Road,
London SW1V 2SA

Vintage Classics is part of the Penguin Random House group of companies
whose addresses can be found at global.penguinrandomhouse.com.

Penguin
Random House
UK

Copyright © Martin Secker & Warburg Ltd 1960

First published in France as *Claudine amoureuse*,
then as *Claudine en ménage*, in 1902
This translation first published in Great Britain
by Martin Secker & Warburg in 1960
First published by Vintage Classics in 2001

www.vintage-books.co.uk

A CIP catalogue record for this book is available
from the British Library

ISBN 9780099422495

Printed and bound in Great Britain by Clays Ltd, Elcograf S.p.A.

Penguin Random House is committed to a sustainable future
for our business, our readers and our planet. This book is
made from Forest Stewardship Council® certified paper.

PREFACE

I have told in *Mes Apprentissages* how, some two years after our marriage, therefore about 1895, Monsieur Willy said to me one day:

'You ought to jot down on paper some memories of the Primary School. I might be able to make something out of them . . . Don't be afraid of racy details.'

This curious and still comparatively unknown man, who put his name to I know not how many volumes without having written a single one of them, was constantly on the look-out for new talents for his literary factory. It was not in the least surprising that he should have extended his investigations as far as his own home.

'I was recovering from a long and serious illness which had left my mind and body lazy. But, having found at a stationer's some exercise-books like the ones I had at school, and bought them again, their cream-laid pages, ruled in grey, with red margins, their black linen spines, and their covers bearing a medallion and an ornate title *Le Calligraphe* gave my fingers back a kind of itch for doing "lines", for the passivity of a set task. A certain watermark, seen through the cream-laid paper, made me feel six years younger. On a stub of a desk, the window behind me, one shoulder askew and my knees crossed, I wrote with application and indifference . . .

'When I had finished, I handed over to my husband a closely-written manuscript which respected the margins. He skimmed through it and said:

'"I made a mistake, this can't be of the slightest use . . ."

'Released, I went back to the sofa, to the cat, to books, to silence, to a life that I tried to make pleasant for myself and that I did not know was unhealthy for me.

'The exercise-books remained for two years at the bottom of a drawer. One day Willy decided to tidy up the contents of his desk.

'The appalling counter-like object of sham ebony with a crimson baize top displayed its deal drawers and disgorged bundles of old papers and once again we saw the forgotten exercise-books in which I had scribbled: *Claudine à l'école*.

'"Fancy," said Monsieur Willy. "I thought I had put them in the waste-paper basket."

'He opened one exercise-book and turned over the pages:

'"It's charming . . ."

'He opened a second exercise-book, and said no more – a third, then a fourth . . .

'"Good Lord," he muttered, "I'm an utter imbecile . . ."

'He swept up the exercise-books haphazard, pounced on his flat-brimmed hat and rushed off to a publisher . . . And that was how I became a writer.'

But that was also how I very nearly missed ever becoming a writer. I lacked the literary vocation and it is probable that I should never have produced another line if, after the success of *Claudine à l'école*, other imposed tasks had not, little by little, got me into the habit of writing.

Claudine à l'école appeared in 1900, published by Paul Ollendorff, bearing Willy's sole name as the author. In the interval, I had to get back to the job again to put a little 'spice' into my text.

'Couldn't you,' Willy said to me, 'hot this – these childish reminiscences up a little? For example, a too passionate friendship between Claudine and one of her schoolmates . . . And then some dialect, lots of dialect words . . . Some naughty pranks . . . You see what I mean?'

The pliancy of extreme youth is only equalled by its lack of scruples. What was the extent of Willy's collaboration? The manuscripts furnish a partial answer to a question that has been asked a hundred times. Out of the four *Claudine* books, only the manuscripts of *Claudine en ménage* and *Claudine s'en va* have been saved from the destruction which Willy ordered Paul Barlet to carry out. Paul Barlet, known as Paul Héon – secretary, friend, Negro and extremely honourable man – suspended the execution, which had begun to be carried out, and brought me what remained, which I still possess.

Turning over the pages of those exercise-books is not without interest. Written entirely in my handwriting, a very fine writing appears at distant intervals, changing a word, adding a pun or a very sharp rebuke. Likewise one could also read (in *Claudine en ménage* and *Claudine s'en va*) two more important re-written passages pasted over the original which I am omitting in the present edition.

The success of the *Claudine* books was, for the period, very great. It inspired fashions, plays, and beauty-products. Being honourable, and above all indifferent, I kept silent about the truth, which did not become known till very much later. Nevertheless, it is today for the first time that the *Claudine* books appear under the single name of their single author. I should also be glad if, henceforth, *La Retraite sentimentale* – a pretty title suggested by Alfred Vallette – were considered as the last book in the *Claudine* series. The reader will find this far more satisfactory from the point of view of both logic and convenience.

COLETTE

ONE

DEFINITELY, THERE IS something wrong with our married life. Renaud knows nothing about it yet; how should he know?

We have been home for six weeks now. It is over, that lazy, feverish, vagabond life that lasted for fifteen months and in which our wanderings took us from the rue de Bassano to Montigny, from Montigny to Bayreuth, from Bayreuth to a village in Baden that I thought at first, to Renaud's huge delight, was called 'Forellen-Fischerei' because an enormous signboard above the river announces you can catch trout there and I don't know German.

Last winter, in a thoroughly hostile mood and clinging tight to Renaud's arm, I saw the Mediterranean. A cold wind was brushing it up the wrong way and it was lit by a thin, harsh sun. Too many parasols, too many hats and faces ruined this meretricious south of France for me. What ruined it most of all was the inevitable meeting with first one, then at least a dozen, of Renaud's friends; with families whom he provided with complimentary tickets; with ladies at whose houses he dined: this appalling man makes himself agreeable to everyone and puts himself out most for the people he knows least. As he explains, with impudent charm, it is not worth while doing violence to one's nature to please one's real friends, since one's sure of them anyway . . .

My puzzled simplicity has never been able to see the point of those winters on the Côte d'Azur where lace frocks shiver under sable stoles!

Moreover, the abuse I showered on Renaud and the abuse

1

he showered on me overstrained my nerves and made me ill able to bear the petty irritations of everyday life. After being dragged from pillar to post in a half-painful, half-delicious state of physical intoxication and a kind of giddy daze, I ended up by demanding mercy and rest and a fixed abode. Well, here I am back at home! So what is it that I need? What is it I still feel lacking?

Let's try and put a little order into this hotch-potch of memories still so recent, yet already so remote.

What a fantastic comedy my wedding-day was! By the time that Thursday arrived, three weeks of being engaged to this Renaud whom I love to distraction, with his embarrassing eyes, his still more embarrassing (though restrained) gestures, and his lips, always in quest of a new place to kiss, had made my face as sharp as a she-cat's on heat. I could make no sense at all of his reserve and abstention during that time! I would have been entirely his, the moment he wanted it, and he was perfectly aware of this. And yet, with too epicurean a concern for his happiness – and for mine? – he kept us in a state of exhausting virtue. His uncontrolled Claudine often gave him angry glances after too brief a kiss, broken off before the proper time. 'But, goodness, in a week's time or less – what difference does it make? You're exciting me for nothing, you're wearing me out with frustration . . .' With no mercy for either of us, he left me, against my will, completely intact until after that slap-dash wedding.

Genuinely annoyed by the necessity of informing His Worship the Mayor and His Reverence the parish priest of my decision to live with Renaud, I refused to help Papa or anyone else in any way at all. Renaud dealt with the matter with expert patience; Papa with unwonted, furious, ostentatious zeal. Mélie alone, radiant at being present at the climax of a love-story, sang and daydreamed at the window overlooking the gloomy little courtyard. Fanchette, followed by Limaçon, still unsteady on his legs and 'fairer than a son of Phtah', sniffed at open cardboard boxes, new materials, and long gloves that made her retch slightly and diligently kneaded my white tulle veil with her front paws.

This pear-shaped ruby that hangs round my neck on such a thin gold chain was given to me by Renaud two days before our wedding. How well I remember his bringing it! Enchanted by its clear-wine colour, I held it up against the light, at eye-level, to admire it, with my other hand resting on Renaud's shoulder as he knelt in front of me.

'Claudine, you're squinting, like Fanchette when she's after a fly.'

Without listening to him, I suddenly put the ruby in my mouth, 'because it ought to melt and taste like a raspberry fruit-drop'! Renaud, baffled by this new way of appreciating precious stones, brought me sweets the following day. Honestly, they gave me as much pleasure as the jewel.

On the great morning, I woke up irritable and surly. I raged against the Town Hall and the Church, the weight of my long-trained dress, the scalding chocolate, and Mélie, who had put on her purple cashmere at seven o'clock and kept gloating, 'My precious, what a time you're going to have!' I raged against those people who were going to come: Maugis and Robert Parville, Renaud's witnesses, Aunt Cœur in Chantilly lace, Marcel, whose father had forgiven him – on purpose to annoy and make fun of him, I believe – and my own witnesses: a very eminent (and very dirty) malacologist whose name I have never discovered, and Monsieur Maria! Papa, serenely forgetful, saw nothing in the least odd in this remarkable devotion on the part of my martyred suitor.

And Claudine, ready long before the time, a little sallow in her white dress and precariously balanced veil – this short hair can be a nuisance at times – sat beside the basket where Fanchette was having her stomach massaged by her striped Limaçon, thinking: 'It revolts me, this wedding! The ideal thing would have been to have had him here, for the two of us to have dinner and then lock ourselves up in this little room where I've gone to sleep thinking of him, where I've thought of him and not been able to go to sleep, and . . . But my little four-poster bed would be too small . . .'

Renaud's arrival, and his slightly flurried gestures, did nothing to drive away these preoccupations. Then, at the urgent request of Monsieur Maria who was going demented, we had to rout out Papa and hurry him up. My noble father, surpassing himself in a manner worthy of the rare occasion, had quite simply forgotten that I was getting married; we discovered him in a dressing-gown (at ten minutes to twelve!) calmly smoking his pipe. He greeted the unfortunate Maria with these memorable words:

'Come along in, Maria. You're devilish late today, just when we've got a very difficult chapter. What's the idea of turning up in dress clothes? You look like a waiter!'

'But, Monsieur . . . Monsieur . . . Mademoiselle Claudine's wedding . . . We're only waiting for you . . .'

'Hell!' replied Papa, consulting his watch instead of the calendar. 'Hell! Are you sure it's today? If you go on ahead, they can begin without me.'

Robert Parville bewildered as a lost poodle because he was not trotting at the heels of his mistress; Maugis glazed with mock solemnity; Monsieur Maria pale as death; Aunt Cœur supercilious, and Marcel stiffly formal – they hardly constituted a crowd, did they? To me, there seemed to be at least fifty of them in the poky flat! Isolated under my veil, I was acutely conscious of my failing, twittering nerves . . .

What followed gave me the impression of one of those confused and muddled dreams in which you feel as if your feet were tied together. A pink and purple ray falling on my white gloves through the stained-glass windows; my nervous laugh in the sacristy when Papa insisted on signing his name twice on the same page, 'because my first flourish isn't impressive enough'. A stifling sensation of unreality; Renaud himself far away and insubstantial . . .

When we returned home, Renaud, thoroughly anxious at the sight of my drawn, unhappy face, questioned me tenderly. I shook my head, saying, 'I don't feel much more married than I did this morning. What about you?' His moustache quivered and, at that, I blushed and shrugged my shoulders.

I wanted to get out of that ridiculous dress and they left me to myself. My darling Fanchette found me easier to recognize in a pink linen blouse and a white serge skirt. 'Fanchette, am I going to leave you? It's the first time ever . . . I've got to . . . I don't want to drag you about in railway trains, along with

4

your precious child.' A slight desire to cry, an indefinable uneasiness, a painful contraction of the ribs. 'Oh, let my beloved take me quickly and deliver me from this idiotic apprehension which is neither fear nor modesty. How late night comes in July, how this white sun makes my temples throb!'

At nightfall, my husband – my husband! – took me away. The noise of the rubber-tyred wheels did not stop me from hearing my heart-beats and I clenched my teeth so tight that his kiss did not unclench them.

In the rue de Bassano, I hardly caught more than a glimpse of that flat 'too like an eighteenth-century engraving' that he had hitherto refused to let me enter. The only light came from shaded writing-lamps placed on the tables. To intoxicate myself still more, I breathed in that smell of light tobacco and Russian leather that permeates Renaud's clothes and his long moustache.

I seem to be still there, I can see myself, I *am* there.

So, the moment had come? What should I do? For a split second, I thought of Luce. Without realizing it, I removed my hat. I took my loved one's hand to reassure myself and I gazed at him. Carelessly, he threw off his hat and gloves and drew back a little, with a trembling sigh. I looked lovingly at his beautiful dark eyes and his arched nose and his faded gold hair that the wind had artfully ruffled. I went up close to him, but he retreated mischievously and contemplated me from a little distance, while all my splendid courage drained away. I clasped my hands.

'Oh! Please do be quick!'

Alas, I did not realize how funny that remark was.

He sat down.

'Come here, Claudine.'

Sitting on his knees, he could hear that I was breathing too fast; his voice became tender.

'Are you my very own?'

'You know I am. I've been yours for so long.'

'You're not frightened?'

'No; I'm not frightened. To begin with, I know everything!'

'What, everything?'

He slid me down, so that I lay on his knees, and bent over my mouth. I put up no defence and let his lips drink deep. I wanted to cry. At least, I felt as if I wanted to cry.

'You know everything, my darling little girl, and you're still not frightened?'

I almost shouted:

'No! . . .'

Yet, all the same, I was and I clung desperately round his neck. With one hand, he was already trying to unhook my blouse. I sprang to my feet.

'No! All by myself!'

Why? I have no idea why. A last vestige of the impulsive Claudine? Completely naked, I would have gone straight to his arms, but I didn't want him to undress me.

With clumsy haste, I undid my clothes and scattered them everywhere, kicking my shoes in the air, picking up my petticoat between two of my toes, and flinging away my corsets, all without one glance at Renaud sitting there in front of me. I had nothing on now but my little chemise and I said: 'There!' with bold defiance as, with my usual gesture, I rubbed the imprint the stays had left round my waist.

Renaud did not move. He merely thrust his head forward, gripped both arms of his chair and stared at me. The heroic Claudine, panic-stricken by that stare, fled in terror and flung herself on the bed – on the bed that was still fully made.

He came and lay on it with me. He held me close, so tense that I could almost hear his muscles quivering. Fully dressed, he embraced me and held me down on it – heavens, whatever was he waiting for to get undressed himself? – and his mouth and his hands forced me to stay there, without his body touching me, from my shuddering revolt to my wild consent, to the shameful moan of voluptuous pleasure I would have liked to hold back out of pride. Only after that did he fling off his clothes, as I had done mine, and laugh mercilessly to annoy an angry and humiliated Claudine. But he demanded nothing, only freedom to give me all the caresses I needed to send me to sleep, in the small hours, still lying on the fully made bed.

I was grateful to him later on – very grateful indeed – for

such active self-denial, for such stoical and frustrated patience. I made up to him for it, when, tamed and curious, I would avidly watch his eyes glaze as he tensely watched mine glaze too. Moreover, for a long time, I retained – and, to tell the truth, I still retain – a slight terror of . . . how can I put it? I think 'marital duty' is the usual term. This potent Renaud made me think, by analogy, of that great gawk Anaïs, who had a mania for cramming her large hands into gloves too tight for them. Apart from that, everything is perfect; everything is even a little too perfect. It is pleasant to begin in complete ignorance and then to learn so many reasons for giving nervous laughs and nervous cries, for uttering little muffled groans, with our toes curled up with tension.

The only caress I have never been able to grant my husband is to use the familiar *tu*. I always use the formal *vous*, on every possible occasion, even when I am imploring him, even when I am consenting, even when the exquisite torture of suspense forces me to speak in jerks, in a voice that is not my own. But isn't this calling him *vous* a special, unique caress from this Claudine who is rather uncivilized and apt to be lavish with *tu*?

He is handsome, I swear he is! His dark, smooth skin glides over mine. Where his great arms join his shoulders, there is a feminine, cushioned roundness where I lay my head, night and morning, for a long while.

And his hair, the colour of a grebe's plumage, his slender knees, his slow-breathing chest, marked with two dark brown specks, the whole of that tall body where I have made so many exciting discoveries! I often tell him, sincerely: 'I do think you're marvellous to look at!' He holds me very tight and says: 'Claudine, Claudine, I'm old!' And his eyes darken with such poignant regret that I stare at him, uncomprehending.

'Ah! Claudine, if I'd known you ten years ago!'

'You'd have known the inside of a law-court if you had! Besides, you were only a young man then, a horrid, filthy brute of a young man who made women cry, while I . . .'

'*You* wouldn't have known Luce.'

'Do you imagine I miss her?'

'At this very moment, no . . . don't shut your eyes, I

implore you, I forbid you to . . . That look in them belongs to me . . .'

'So does my whole self!'

My whole self? No. That is the flaw.

I have evaded this certainty as long as I could. I hoped so ardently that Renaud's will would curb mine, that his tenacity would eventually overcome my fits of rebellion; in short, that his character would match the expression of his eyes, accustomed to command and to fascinate. Renaud's will, Renaud's tenacity! He is suppler than a flame, just as burning, just as flickering; he envelops me without dominating me. Alas! Are you to remain your own mistress for ever, Claudine?

All the same, he knows how to subjugate my slim, golden body, this skin that clings to my muscles and refuses to obey the pressure of hands, this little girl's head with the hair cut like a little boy's . . . Why do they have to lie, his dominating eyes, his stubborn nose and his attractive, clean-shaven chin that he displays as coquettishly as a woman?

I am gentle with him, and I make myself small; I bend my neck meekly under his kisses; I demand nothing and I avoid any kind of argument in the virtuous fear of seeing him give in to me at once and smiling a too-facile *yes* with his good-natured mouth. He has no authority except when he is making love.

I realize that, at least, is something.

I told him about Luce, every single detail, almost in the hope of seeing him frown and get angry and ply me with furious questions . . . Oh dear no, not at all! On the contrary, even. He plied me with questions, yes, but not furious ones. And I cut short my answers because my mind was harking back to his son, Marcel (it irritated me to remember how that boy used to harass me with questions), but certainly not out of defiance. For, if I have not found my master, I have found my friend and ally.

All this hotch-potch of feelings would get short-shrift from Papa. Contemptuous of the psychological mix-ups of a daughter who quibbled and dissected and pretended to be a complex person, his answer would be: 'The bloody little fool's got a bee in her bonnet and nothing will stop it buzzing!'

My admirable father! Since my marriage, I haven't thought enough about him, or about Fanchette. But, for months, Renaud has loved me too much, taken me about too much, made me too drunk with landscapes, too dazed with movement and new skies and unknown towns . . . Little knowing his Claudine, he has often smiled in amazement at seeing me more impressed by a landscape than a picture, more excited by a tree than by a museum, or by a river than a jewel. He had a great deal to teach me and I have learnt a great deal.

Sexual pleasure appeared to me like some overwhelming, almost sombre marvel. When Renaud, seeing me suddenly still and serious, would question me anxiously, I turned red and answered, without looking at him: 'I can't tell you . . .' And I would be forced to explain myself without words to that redoubtable questioner who battens on looking at me, who watches every nuance of shame on my face and finds exquisite pleasure in heightening it.

It would seem that for him – and I feel this is what separates us – sexual pleasure is made up of desire, perversity, lively curiosity, and deliberate licentiousness. To him pleasure is something gay and lenient and facile, whereas it shatters me and plunges me into a mysterious despair that I seek and also fear. When Renaud is already smiling as he lies panting beside me, no longer holding me in his arms, I am still hiding my terrified eyes and my ecstatic mouth in my hands, however much he tries to stop me. It is only a little while after that I go and huddle up against his reassuring shoulder and complain to my friend of the too-delicious pain my lover has caused me.

Sometimes, I try to persuade myself that perhaps love is still too new for me, whereas, for Renaud, it has lost its bitterness. I doubt if this is true. We shall never think the same about love, apart from the great affection that drew us together and still binds us.

In a restaurant, the other night, he smiled at a slim, dark woman who was dining alone and whose beautiful made-up eyes responded willingly.

'Do you know her?'

'Who? The lady? No, darling. But she's got a very pretty figure, don't you think?'

'Is that the only reason why you're looking at her?'

'Of course, my precious child. That doesn't shock you, I trust?'

'No, not a bit. Only . . . I don't like her smiling at you.'

'Oh, Claudine!' he pleaded, putting his swarthy face close to me. 'Do let me go on believing that people can still look at your old husband without repulsion; he so much needs to have a little self-confidence!' He added, tossing his fine, light hair, 'The day when women stop looking at me at all, there'll be nothing for me but to . . .'

'But whatever does it matter about other women? Because *I* shall always love you.'

'Hush, Claudine,' he cut in deftly. 'Heaven preserve me from seeing you become a unique monstrosity!'

There you are! Talking of me, he says *women*; do I say *men* when I'm talking of him? Oh, I know the answer. The habit of living in the public eye and having constant illicit love-affairs affects a man, subjects him to humiliating worries unknown to little brides of nineteen.

I could not resist saying spitefully:

'No wonder Marcel's like a flirtatious girl who can't live without admiration. He's obviously inherited your temperament.'

'Oh, Claudine! Don't you like my defects?' he asked a little sadly. 'Certainly, I can't see where else he got them from . . . At least, you must admit that I exploit my charms for less perverse reasons than he does!'

How quickly he switched back to light-hearted frivolity! I believe that, had he answered me sharply, knitting those beautiful eyebrows, like the velvet lining of a ripe chestnut-burr, 'That's enough, Claudine. Marcel doesn't come into this,' I should have begun to feel a great joy and a little of that timid respect that I want to feel for Renaud and cannot.

Rightly or wrongly, I need to respect, to be a little afraid of the man I love. I was a stranger to fear for as long as I was a stranger to love and I should have liked both to have come together.

My memories of the past fifteen months mill about in my head like specks of dust in a dark room barred by one shaft of sunshine. One after the other they pass into the beam, glitter there for a second while I smile or pout at them, then go back into the shadow.

When I returned to France, three months ago, I wanted to see Montigny again. But this deserves what Luce calls commencing at the beginning.

Eighteen months ago, Mélie hastened to announce loudly and triumphantly to Montigny that I was getting married 'to ever such a fine man, a bit on the old side, but still good and lusty'.

Papa dispatched a few printed announcements at random, one of them to Darjeau the carpenter 'because he made a devilish good job of the packing-cases for my books'. And I myself sent two, with the addresses inscribed in my best handwriting, to Mademoiselle Sergent and to her disgusting little Aimée. This earned me a somewhat unexpected letter.

'My dear child,' wrote back Mademoiselle Sergent, 'I am sincerely happy' (keep a straight face, Claudine!) 'about this marriage of affection' (her language goes beyond the bounds of decency) 'which will be a sure safeguard against a slightly dangerous independence. Do not forget that the School eagerly awaits a visit from you, should you return, as I hope, to see a part of the country that so many memories must have endeared to your heart.'

This final irony was blunted by the universal kindliness I felt for everything and everyone just then. All that persisted in my mind was amused surprise and the desire to see Montigny again – oh, woods that had enchanted me! – with sadder, more sophisticated eyes.

And, as we were returning from Germany via Switzerland last September, I begged Renaud to agree to break our journey and spend twenty-four hours with me in the very heart of Fresnois, at Montigny's mediocre inn, Lange's, in the Place de l'Horloge.

He consented at once, as he always consents.

To re-live those days, I have only to close my eyes for a minute.

Two

IN THE SLOW train that pottered irresolutely through that green, undulating countryside, I thrilled at the well-known names of the deserted little stations. Good heavens! After Blégeau and Saint-Farcy, it would be Montigny and I should see the ruined tower . . . I was so excited that my calves prickled with nerves: I stood up in the compartment, clutching the cloth arm-straps with both hands. Renaud, who was watching me, with his travelling-cap pulled down over his eyes, came and joined me at the window.

'Darling bird, are you flustered at getting so near your old nest? . . . Claudine, do answer . . . I'm jealous . . . I don't like seeing you so tensely silent except in my arms.'

I reassured him with a smile, and once again I scanned the forest-fleeced back of the hills as they fled whirling past.

'Ah!'

With my outstretched finger, I pointed to the tower, its crumbling red-brown stone draped with ivy, and to the village that cascades below it and looks as if it were pouring out of it. The sight of it gave me such a fierce, sweet pain that I leant on Renaud's shoulder . . .

Broken summit of the tower, mass of round-headed trees, how could I ever have left you? And must I feast my eyes on you only to go away and leave you again?

I threw my arms round my husband's neck; it was to him I must look now for my strength and my motive for living. It was for him to enchant me, to hold me fast; that was what I hoped, that was what I wanted.

The gate-keeper's little pink house at the level-crossing whisked by, then the goods station – I recognized the foreman! – and we jumped out on the platform. Renaud had already put the suitcase and my handbag into the one and only omnibus while I was still standing rooted to the spot, silently registering the humps and the holes and the landmarks of the beloved shrunken horizon. There, right above us, was the Fredonnes wood that joins up with the Vallées one . . . that yellow, sandy serpent is the path to Vrimes, how narrow it was! And it would no longer take me over to see the girl who made her First Communion with me, my delicious Claire. Oh! They had cut down the Corbeaux wood without my permission! Now you could see its rough skin, all bare . . . Joy, joy, to see Quail Mountain again, blue and misty: on sunny days it was clothed in a rainbow haze but you can see it close and clear when it's going to rain. It is full of fossil shells and purple thistles and harsh, sapless flowers and haunted by little butterflies with pearly blue wings, tortoise-shells speckled with orange half-moons like orchids, and heavy Camberwell beauties in dark, gilded velvet . . .

'Claudine! Don't you think sooner or later we'll have to face climbing into this bone-shaking contraption?' asked Renaud, who was laughing at my blissful stupor.

I got into the bus with him. Nothing had changed; old Racalin was drunk, as in the old days. Immutably drunk, he sent his creaking vehicle lurching from one ditch to another with authoritative self-assurance.

I scrutinized every hedge, every turning, ready to protest if they had touched *my* country. I said nothing, not another word, till we reached the first tumbledown cottages at the bottom of the steep slope, and then I exclaimed:

'But the cats won't be able to sleep in Bardin's hay-loft any more. There's a new door!'

'"Pon my soul, you're right,' agreed Renaud, impressed. 'That brute of a Bardin's had a new door put in!' My previous dumbness burst into a spate of gay, idiotic chatter.

'Renaud, Renaud, look quick, we're going to go right past the gate of the castle! It's deserted; we'll see the tower in a minute: Oh, there's old Madame Sainte-Albe on her doorstep!

13

I'm sure she saw me; she'll go and tell the whole street . . . quick, quick turn round; there, those two tree-tops above old Madame Adolphe's roof, they're the big fir-trees in the garden, *my* fir-trees, my very own ones . . . They haven't grown; that's good . . . Who on earth's that girl I don't know?'

Apparently I asked this last in a tone of such comical asperity that Renaud roared with laughter and displayed all his white, square teeth. But there were snags ahead; we had got to spend the night under Lange's roof and my husband might well laugh less light-heartedly up there, in the gloomy inn . . .

Mercifully, it was all right! He found the room tolerable, in spite of the tent-shaped bed-curtains, the minute wash-basin, and the coarse sheets that were greyish, but, thank heaven, very clean.

Renaud, excited by the poverty of the setting, by all the childishness that Montigny brought out in Claudine, flung his arms round me from behind and tried to pull me on to the bed. But I wouldn't let him . . . the time would pass too quickly.

'Renaud, Renaud, dear, it's six o'clock. *Please* come over to the School and let's give Mademoiselle a surprise before dinner!'

'Alas!' he sighed, anything but resigned. 'That's what comes of marrying a stuck-up little child of nature – she deceives you with a country town numbering 1,847 inhabitants!'

A dab of the brush on my short hair (the dry air made it light and fluffy), an uneasy glance in the mirror – had I aged in eighteen months? – and we were outside in the Place de l'Horloge. It is so steep that, on market days, any number of little stalls find it impossible to keep their balance, turn *oopsidaisy* and collapse with a tremendous clatter.

Thanks to my husband, thanks to my shorn locks (feeling a trifle jealous of myself, I thought of the long chestnut ringlets that used to dance well below my waist), nobody recognized me and I was able to take it all in at leisure.

'Oh, Renaud, just imagine, that woman with a baby in her arms, that's Célénie Nauphely!'

14

'The one who used to suck her sister's milk?'

'None other. Now she's the one who's being sucked. Lawks a mercy, did you ever? It's disgusting!'

'Why disgusting?'

'I don't know. Little Madame Chou has still got the same peppermints in her shop. Perhaps she doesn't sell any more now that Luce has gone . . .'

The main street – nearly ten feet wide – runs down so steeply that Renaud asked where they sold alpenstocks here. But Claudine danced on, her straw boater over one eye, dragging him along by his little finger. As the two strangers passed by, the doorways filled with familiar and rather malevolent faces; I could put a name to all of them, check up all their wrinkles and blemishes.

'I'm living in a drawing by Huard,' declared Renaud.

An angrily exaggerated Huard, he might even have said. I had not remembered that the slope of the whole village was so abrupt and steep, or the streets so flinty, or old Sandré's hunting costume so aggressively warlike . . . Had the aged Lourd really been as smiling and drooling in his dotage when I saw him last? At the corner of the rue Bel-Air, I stopped and laughed out aloud:

'Good Lord! Madame Armand is still wearing her curl-papers! She twists them up at night when she goes to bed, forgets to take them out in the morning and then it's too late, it's not worth the bother, so she keeps them in the following night. Next morning, the same thing happens and so it goes on. I've never seen her without them, writhing like worms on her greasy forehead! . . . For ten years, Renaud, just here, where these three streets meet, I used to admire a wonderful man called Hébert who was Mayor of Montigny, though he could hardly sign his name. He used to attend all the Council meetings, nodding his fine official head – he had a red face and almost white flaxen hair – and making speeches that have remained famous. For example: "To make a gutter in the rue des Fours-Baneaux? *Tattistykestion*, as the English say." Between sessions he used to stand here at the crossroads, look-ing purple in winter and scarlet in summer, and observing – what? Nothing! It was his entire occupation. He died of it . . .'

15

My husband's indulgent laugh was growing a trifle strained. Was he beginning to find me a bore? No; he was only feeling a jealous resentment at seeing me completely reabsorbed in the past.

And then, at the bottom of the hill, the street opened out into a roughly cobbled square. A stone's-throw away, behind iron-grey railings, loomed the huge square block of the slate-roofed School, its whiteness hardly soiled by three winters and four summers.

'Claudine, is that the barracks?'

'No, of course not! It's the School!'

'Poor kids . . .'

'Why "poor kids"? I assure you we were anything but bored there.'

'*You* weren't, you little she-devil. But the others! Are we going in? Is one allowed to visit the prisoners at any time?'

'Wherever were you brought up, Renaud? Don't you know that this is the holidays?'

'No! You mean to say you dragged me here just to see this empty gaol? Was that the exciting prospect all the throbbing and panting was about, you fussy little steam-engine?'

'You lumbering old push-cart!' I said triumphantly. A year of foreign travel has been enough to enrich my native vocabulary with 'typically Parisian' insults.

'Suppose I deprived you of pudding?'

'Suppose I put you on a diet?'

Suddenly serious, I fell silent. As I put my hand on the latch of the heavy gate, I had felt it resist, just as in the old days . . .

By the pump in the courtyard, the little rusty mug – the same one – hung from its chain. Two years ago, the walls had been all white and chalky; now they were scratched, shoulder-high, as if by the nails of restive prisoners. But the thin grass of the summer holidays was pushing up between the bricks of the gutter.

Not a soul in sight.

With Renaud following meekly behind me, I climbed the little flight of six steps, opened a glass-topped door, and walked along the paved, echoing corridor that runs from the playground to the three downstairs classrooms. That gust of fetid coolness – hasty sweeping, ink, chalk-dust, blackboards washed with dirty sponges – stifled me with a very strange feeling. Surely at any moment, the importunate, loving little ghost of Luce, in her black apron, would slip round the corner of that wall, swift and light on her rope-soled shoes, and bury her face in my skirts?

I gave a start and felt my cheeks quiver; swift and silent on rope-soled shoes, a little ghost in a black apron was pushing open the playground door . . . But no, it was not Luce; a pretty little face that I had never seen before was staring at me with limpid eyes. Reassured, and feeling almost at home, I went forward:

'Mmmzelle anywhere about?'

'I don't know, Mada . . . Mademoiselle. Upstairs, I expect.'

'Right, thanks. But . . . aren't you on holiday?'

'I'm one of the boarders spending the summer holidays in Montigny.'

She was utterly charming, the boarder spending the summer holidays in Montigny! Her chestnut plait fell forward over her black apron as she drooped her head, hiding a fresh, sweet mouth and reddish-brown eyes that were lovely rather than lively – the eyes of a doe watching a motor-car go by.

A biting voice (oh, how well I recognized it) interrupted us from the staircase:

'Pomme, whoever are you talking to?'

'Somebody, Mmmzelle!' cried the innocent little thing, running off up the stairs that led to the private rooms and dormitory.

I turned round to give Renaud a laughing look. He was interested, his nose was twitching.

'Hear that, Claudine? Pomme! Someone'll eat her up with a name like that. Lucky I'm only an old gentleman past the age! . . .'

'Shut up, schoolgirl's dream! Someone's coming.'

A rapid whispering, a brisk step coming downstairs, and Mademoiselle Sergent appeared. Dressed in black, her red hair blazing in the setting sun, she was so like herself that I wanted to bite her and fling myself round her neck for the

17

sake of all the Past she brought back to me in that direct, black gaze of hers.

She paused for a couple of seconds; that was enough, she had seen everything; seen that I was Claudine, that my hair was cut short, that my eyes were bigger and my face smaller, that Renaud was my husband and that he was still (I could read her thoughts!) a fine figure of a man.

'Claudine! Oh! you haven't changed a bit . . . Whyever didn't you warn me you were coming? How d'you do, Monsieur? Fancy this child not telling me a word about your visit! Don't you think she deserves two hundred lines as a punishment? Is she still as much of a young terror as ever? Are you quite sure she was fit to get married?'

'No, Mademoiselle, not at all sure. Only I hadn't enough time ahead of me and I wanted to avoid being married on my death-bed.'

Things were going well; they'd 'clicked'; they'd get on with each other. Mademoiselle likes handsome males, even if she doesn't make much use of them. I left them to enjoy each other's company.

While they were chatting, I went off to ferret about in the Senior Classroom, hunting for my desk, the one Luce used to share with me. I ended by discovering under all the spilt ink, under the new and old scars, the remains of an inscription cut with a knife . . . *uce* et *Claudi* . . . 15th February 189 . . .

Did I put my lips to it? I will not admit it . . . Looking at it so close to, my mouth must have brushed that scarred wood. But, if I wanted to be absolutely truthful, I should say, now that I realize it, that I was very harsh in my repudiation of poor Luce's slavish affection. And I should say that it took me two years, a husband, and the return to that school to understand the true worth of her humility, her freshness, and her gentle, frankly-offered perversity.

The voice of Mademoiselle Sergent roughly banished my dream.

'Claudine! I presume you've taken leave of your senses? Your husband informs me that your suitcases are over at Lange's!'

'Well, where else should they be? I couldn't leave my nightdress in the station cloakroom!'

'That's simply absurd! I've heaps of empty beds upstairs, not to mention Mademoiselle Lanthenay's room . . .'

'What! Isn't Mademoiselle Aimée here?' I exclaimed, sounding far too surprised.

'Now, now, where's your head?'

She came close to me and ran her hand over my hair with thinly veiled irony.

'During the summer holidays, Madame Claudine, the assistant mistresses return to their own homes.'

Bother! And I'd been counting on the spectacle of the Sergent–Lanthenay *ménage* to edify and delight Renaud! I had imagined that even the holidays could not separate this exceptionally united couple. Ah, well, that little bitch of an Aimée wouldn't trail around long with her family! I understood now why Mademoiselle had welcomed us with such surprising affability; it was because Renaud and I were not disturbing any intimate scene . . . what a pity!

'Thank you for your offer, Mmmzelle; I'd be delighted to recover a little of my lost youth by spending the night at school. Who on earth is the little green apple – I mean that child Pomme – we met just now?'

'A noodle who's failed her oral in the elementary exams, after having asked for an exemption. An absurd business. The little fool's fifteen. She's spending her holidays here as a punishment, but otherwise she doesn't seem in the least upset. I've got two others like her upstairs, two girls from Paris rusticating here till October . . . You'll see them all later . . . but come along first and get settled in . . .'

She slipped me a sidelong look and asked in her most natural voice:

'Would you like to sleep in Mademoiselle Aimée's room?'

'I should love to sleep in Mademoiselle Aimée's room!'

Renaud followed us, alert now and enjoying himself. The crude chalk and charcoal drawings fixed to the passage wall with drawing-pins made his nostrils quiver with amusement and his moustache twitch ironically.

The favourite bedroom! . . . It had been embellished since my time. That white bed for one and a half people, those liberty draperies at the window, those mantelpiece ornaments (ugh!) in copper and alabaster, the shining order everywhere, and the faint perfume that hovered in the folds of the curtains absorbed me so much I could think of nothing else.

When the door had closed behind Mademoiselle, Renaud turned to me.

'Why, my darling child,' he said, 'these staff bedrooms are very pleasant indeed! They quite reconcile me to your secular school.'

I burst out laughing.

'Oh, my goodness me! You don't really imagine this is the official furniture? Come on, use your memory! I've told you at great length about Aimée and the part that flaunting favourite plays here. The other assistant mistress has to put up with a three-foot iron bedstead, a deal table, and a basin I couldn't drown one of Fanchette's kittens in.'

'Oh! Then you actually mean it's here, in this very room that . . .'

'Yes, of *course* it's here in this very room that . . .'

'Claudine, you can't imagine what a sensational effect this has on me, all that it conjures up . . .'

Oh yes I could; I could imagine it only too well. But I remained resolutely blind and deaf and I studied the scandalous bed with distaste. It might be wide enough for them but not for us. I was going to suffer. Renaud would be unbearably close. I should be hot and I shouldn't be able to spread my legs. And there was that worn hollow in the middle, ugh!

It took the open window and the beloved landscape it framed to restore my good temper. The woods; the narrow, poor-soiled fields, all stubble after the harvest; the Pottery glowing red in the dusk . . .

'Oh, Renaud, look – see that tiled roof over there! They make little glazed brown pots there and two-handled pitchers with indecent little tubular navels . . .'

'Sort of peasant-ware pisspots? I know. Rather charming.'

'Ages ago, when I was quite a little girl, I used to go and see some of the potters and they'd give me little brown pots and cider-mugs. And they used to tell me proudly, waving their hands all covered with wet clay, like gloves: "It's us as does all the pottery for the Adret's Inn in Paris."'

20

'Really, my little curly shepherd-boy? Being an old man, I remember the place. I've drunk once or twice from those cider-mugs without realizing that your slim fingers might have brushed against them. I love you . . .'

A tumult of fresh voices and small, trampling feet drove us apart. The steps in the passage slowed down outside the door; the voices lowered to whisperings; there came two timid knocks.

'Come in!'

Pomme appeared, flushed and overwhelmed with her own importance.

'It's us, with your bags. Old Racalin's just brought these over from Lange's.'

Behind her was a cluster of black aprons; a red-haired child of about ten with a quaint, amusing little face, and a brunette of fourteen or fifteen with an ivory skin and black, luminous, liquid eyes. Frightened by my stare, she shrank aside, disclosing another brunette of the same age, with the same eyes and the same ivory skin . . . How amusing! I caught hold of her sleeve:

'How many copies of this model are there?'

'Only two. She's my sister.'

'I had a sort of vague suspicion she might be . . . You don't come from these parts, I realize that.'

'Oh no! . . . we live in Paris.'

The tone, the little half-suppressed smile of disdainful superiority on the curved mouth – honestly, she was delicious enough to eat!

Pomme was dragging the heavy suitcase. Renaud relieved her of it with zealous eagerness.

'Pomme, how old are you?'

'Fifteen and two months, Monsieur.'

'You're not married, Pomme?'

They all burst out laughing like clucking hens! Pomme split her sides artlessly; the dark-haired, white-skinned sisters managed their mirth more elegantly. And the little thing of ten, buried in her carroty hair, was definitely going to make herself ill with laughing. Splendid! Here was my school, just as I'd always known it!

21

'Pomme,' went on Renaud, without moving a muscle, 'I'm sure you like sweets!'

Pomme gazed at him with her reddish-brown eyes as if she were yielding up her soul to him.

'Oh yes, Monsieur!'

'Good, I'll go and get some. Don't bother, darling. I'll find them perfectly well on my own.'

I remained with the little girls, who scanned the passage nervously, terrified of getting caught in the lady's bedroom. I wanted them to feel relaxed and at home.

'What are your names, you little black-and-white ones?'

'Hélène Jousserand, Madame.'

'Isabelle Jousserand, Madame.'

'Don't call me Madame, silly infants. I'm Claudine. You don't know who Claudine is, do you?'

'Oh, yes we do!' cried Hélène (the younger and prettier). 'Mademoiselle always tells us, when we've done something naughty . . .'

Her sister nudged her; she stopped.

'Go on, go on. You intrigue me! Don't listen to your sister.'

'All right, then; she says: "My word, it's enough to make me wash my hands of the whole place! Anyone would think we were back in the days of Claudine!" Or else: "*That*, young ladies, is worthy of Claudine!"'

I broke into an exultant 'goat dance'.

'What luck! *I'm* the scarecrow, *I'm* the monster, the legendary terror! . . . Am I as ugly as you expected me to be?'

'Oh no,' said little Hélène, tenderly and shyly, quickly veiling her soft eyes behind a double fence of lashes.

The caressing spirit of Luce haunted this house. It was possible, too, there were other examples . . . I'd make them talk, these two little girls. We must get the other one out of the way.

'I say, you, go and look outside in the passage and see if I'm there.'

The red-head, devoured with curiosity, looked sullen and refused to budge.

'Nana, will you do as the lady tells you!' cried Hélène Jousserand, quite pink with fury. 'Listen, old thing, if you stay in here, I'll tell Mademoiselle that you take letters from the girl who shares your desk over to the boys' playground. All for filthy bribes in the shape of chocolates!'

The little girl had already vanished. With my arms round the shoulders of the two sisters, I looked at them from close to. Hélène was the more charming, Isabelle the more serious; she had a barely visible down of moustache that would be troublesome later on.

'Hélène, Isabelle, is it a long time since Mademoiselle Aimée went away?'

'It's . . . twelve days,' replied Hélène.

'Thirteen,' corrected Isabelle.

'Tell me, just between us, does she still get on well, *very* well, with Mademoiselle?'

Isabelle blushed, Hélène smiled.

'Right. I don't need to ask any more. That's how things were in my time; this . . . friendship . . . has lasted three years, my children!'

'Oh!' they exclaimed simultaneously.

'Exactly, it's about two years since I left the School, and I saw them together for a whole year . . . a year I'm not likely to forget . . . And, do tell me, is she still pretty, that loathsome little Lanthenay?'

'Yes,' said Isabelle.

'Not as pretty as you,' murmured Hélène, who was beginning to eat out of my hand.

By way of caress, I dug my nails into the nape of her neck, as I used to do to Luce. She did not blink. The atmosphere of this School where I could still assert my power intoxicated me.

Pomme, her arms dangling and her mouth half-open, listened affably, but without real interest. Her mind was elsewhere. Every other second, she leant forward to look through the window and see whether the sweets were coming.

I wanted to know more.

'Hélène, Isabelle, tell me a little of the School news. Who are the seniors in the First Division now?'

'There's . . . Liline, and Mathilde.'

'*No!* Already? Yes, of course, it's two years . . . Is Liline still

23

good-looking? I used to call her the Gioconda. Her green and grey eyes, that silent mouth with the tight corners . . .'

'Oh!' broke in Hélène, pouting her moist pink lips. 'She's not as beautiful as all that – anyway, not this year.'

'Don't you believe her,' Isabelle-the-Downy snapped very quickly. 'She's the best-looking of them all.'

'Coo! Everyone knows why you say that *and* why Mademoiselle won't let you sit next to each other at the evening class any more, even though you're mugging up the same book!'

The elder one's lovely eyes filled with bright tears.

'Will you let your sister alone, you little pest! And you needn't put on that saintly air either! After all, this child's only imitating the example set by Mademoiselle and Aimée . . .'

Inwardly, I was delirious with joy; things were going well, the School had made considerable progress! In my time, Luce was the only one who wrote me love-letters; Anaïs herself had got no further than boys. How charming they were, this new lot! If Doctor Dutertre still carried on his job as Regional Inspector, he had nothing to complain of.

Our group was worth looking at. A brunette to the right, a brunette to the left, Claudine's curly, excited head in the middle, and that fresh Pomme innocently contemplating us . . . bring on the old gentlemen! When I say 'the old gentlemen' . . . I know some, who, though still young . . . It would not be long before Renaud returned.

'Pomme, do go and look out of the window and see if the gentleman with the sweets is coming! . . . Is her name really Pomme?' I asked my pretty Hélène, who was leaning trustfully against my shoulder.

'Yes; her name's Marie Pomme; she's always called "Pomme".'

'Not exactly a brilliant genius, eh?'

'Goodness gracious, no! But she doesn't make a nuisance of herself and she agrees with everybody.'

I went off into a daydream, and they stared at me. Like reassured little animals they investigated everything about me with curious eyes and light paws. 'It curls naturally, doesn't it?' they asked, touching my short hair. Fingering my white buckskin belt, a hand's-breadth wide, with its dull gold buckle, a present – like everything I have – from Renaud, one cried: 'There, you see! *You* insisted broad belts weren't being worn any more.' They studied my stiffly starched butterfly collar, my pale blue linen blouse with its broad tucks . . . Time was slipping by . . . I realized that I was leaving tomorrow; that all this was a brief dream; that I was jealous of a present that was already past and wanted to leave a mark on it. I wanted to imprint a sweet and searing memory on something or on somebody . . . I tightened my arm about Hélène's shoulder and whispered almost inaudibly:

'If I were your school friend, little Hélène, would you love me as much as your sister loves Liline?'

Her Spanish eyes, with their drooping corners, opened wide, as if almost frightened: then the thick lashes were lowered and I felt her shoulders stiffen.

'I don't know yet . . .'

That was enough; I knew.

Pomme, over at the window, burst into shrieks of joy: 'Bags and bags! He's got simply *sacks* of them!'

After this explosion, Renaud's entrance was greeted with a reverent silence. He had bought everything Montigny's modest sweet-shop could provide: from chocolate creams to striped bull's-eyes and English sweets whose smell reminds you of sour cider.

All the same, such a quantity of sweets! . . . I wanted some too! Renaud, who had stopped in the doorway, gazed at our group for a minute with a smile – a smile I had sometimes seen on his face before – and at last took pity on the palpitating Pomme.

'Pomme, which do you like best?'

'All of them!' cried Pomme, intoxicated.

'Oh!' the other two exclaimed indignantly. 'How *can* you!'

'Pomme,' went on Renaud, bubbling over with pleasure, 'I'll give you this bag here, if you'll kiss me . . . You don't mind, Claudine?'

'Heavens, *I* don't care!'

Pomme hesitated for three seconds, torn between her

furious greed and regard for the proprieties. Her frank, red-brown gaze wandered beseechingly to her hostile schoolmates, to me, to heaven, to the bags Renaud was holding out to her at arm's length . . . Then, with the slightly foolish grace of her whole small person, she flung her arms round Renaud's neck, received the bag and went off, scarlet, to open it in a corner . . .

I meanwhile was pillaging a box of chocolates, helped silently, but swiftly, by the pair of sisters. Hélène's small hand went to and fro from the box to her mouth, sure and indefatigable . . . Who would have thought that little mouth could take in so much!

A shrill bell interrupted us and broke off Renaud's contemplative trance. The little girls fled in terror, without saying 'Thank you', without even glancing at us, like thieving cats . . .

Dinner in the refectory amused Renaud prodigiously, but I was slightly bored by it. The uncertain hour, the purple twilight I could feel thickening and falling on the woods . . . I escaped, in spite of myself . . . But my dear man was so happy! Ah, how craftily Mademoiselle had found the right way to arouse his curiosity! Sitting beside Renaud, in this white room, at the table covered with white oilcloth, opposite those pretty little girls, still in their black aprons, who were fiddling disgustedly with their boiled beef after their orgy of sweets, Mademoiselle talked about me. She talked about me, lowering her voice now and then, because of the pricked-up ears of the two little Jousserands were straining in our direction. Wearily, I listened and smiled.

'She was a terrible tomboy, Monsieur, and, for a long time, I didn't know what to do with her. From fourteen to fifteen, she spent most of her time twenty feet above ground and her sole preoccupation appeared to be to display her legs right up to her eyes. I've sometimes seen her show the cruelty children show to grown-up people . . .' (*That was a good one! . . .*) 'She's remained just what she was, a delicious little girl. Although she didn't like me at all, I used to enjoy watching her move . . . such suppleness, such precision of movement. The staircase that leads to this room – I've never seen her come down it except astride the banisters. Monsieur, what an example to the others!'

The perfidiousness of that motherly tone ended up by amusing me and by kindling a well-known dark and dangerous light in Renaud's eyes. He looked at Pomme, but what he was seeing was Claudine, Claudine at fourteen and her legs displayed 'up to the eyes' (up to the eyes, Mademoiselle! The tone of the establishment has risen considerably since I left it). He looked at Hélène and saw Claudine astride a banister rail, Claudine cheeky and defiant, blotched with purple ink-stains. It would be a warm night. And he burst into a nervous laugh when Mademoiselle turned away from him to exclaim: 'Pomme, if you take salt with your fingers again, I shall make you copy out five pages of Blanchet!'

Little Hélène was very silent; she kept trying to catch my eye and avoiding it when she succeeded. Her sister Isabelle was decidedly less pretty; that shadow of a moustache, now that it was no longer silvered by daylight, made her look like a child that has not wiped its mouth properly.

'Mademoiselle,' said Renaud, coming to with a start, 'will you authorize a distribution of sweets tomorrow morning?'

The voracious little red-head, who had licked all the plates clean and eaten up all the crusts during dinner, let out a little yelp of greed. No! said the contemptuous eyes of the three big ones, who were already gorged with sticky filth.

'I authorize it,' replied Mademoiselle. 'They don't deserve anything; they're a lot of ticks. But the circumstances are so exceptional! Well, come along, aren't you going to say thank you, little sillies? Have you lost your tongues? . . . Off to bed with you now! It's nearly nine o'clock.'

'Oh, Mmmzelle, may Renaud see the dormitory before the kids go to bed?'

'Kid yourself! Yes, he may,' she conceded, rising from her chair. 'And you, Miss Untidies, if I find one brush lying about!'

Grey-white, blue-white, yellow-white; the walls, the curtains, the narrow beds that looked like babies swaddled too tight. Renaud sniffed the peculiar smell in the air; the smell of healthy little girls and of sleep, the dry, peppery fragrance of marsh peppermint, a bunch of which hung from the ceiling; his subtle nose analysed, savoured, and took it all in. Mademoiselle, from force of habit, thrust a redoubtable hand under the bolsters in search of booty to confiscate – a half-nibbled tablet of chocolate or an instalment of a forbidden book, serialized in ten-centime paperbacks.

'Did you ever sleep here?' Renaud asked me, very low, drumming his burning fingers on my shoulders.

Mademoiselle's sharp ear caught the question and she forestalled my reply.

'Claudine? Never in her life! And I'm extremely glad she didn't. Whatever state should we have found the dormitory in next day – not to mention the boarders!'

'Not to mention the boarders' – she had actually said that! It was the giddy limit! My modesty was up in arms. I just could not tolerate these broad hints any longer. High time we got off to bed.

'Seen everything you want to see, Renaud?'

'Everything.'

'Then let's go to bed.'

There was much whispering as we turned to go. I could guess pretty well what the little brunettes were muttering: 'I say, is she going to sleep with the gentleman in Mademoiselle Aimée's bed? . . . First time it's ever had even one man in it, Mademoiselle Aimée's bed!'

The sooner we got away, the better. I flashed a smile at little Hélène, who was plaiting her hair for the night, her chin on her shoulder. More than ever, I wanted to be gone.

The cramped, light bedroom, the lamp that gave out too much heat, the pure blue of the night through the window; a cat creeping like a little velvet ghost along the dangerous window-ledge.

The reviving ardour of my lord and master, who had been titillated all the evening by too-youthful Claudines, the nervous excitement that drew the corners of his mouth into a horizontal smile . . .

My own brief slumber, lying on my stomach with my hands clasped behind my back 'like a bound captive', as Renaud says . . .

The dawn that drew me from bed to stand at the window in my nightdress, so as to see the mist sailing over the woods up by Moutiers, so as to hear the little anvil at Choucas from closer to. It rang that morning, as it had rung all those other mornings, a clear G sharp . . .

Every detail of that night is still clear in my mind.

In the school, nothing was stirring yet; it was only six o'clock. But Renaud woke up because he could no longer feel me there in the bed; he listened to the blacksmith's silvery hammering and unconsciously whistled a motif from *Siegfried* . . .

He is not ugly in the morning, and that after all is a great asset in a man! Invariably, he begins by combing his hair over to the left with his fingers, then he flings himself on the water-jug and drinks a huge glass of water. This is quite beyond me! How can anyone drink something cold first thing in the morning? And, since I don't like it, how can *he* possibly like it?

'Claudine, what time are we leaving?'

'I don't know. So soon?'

'So soon. You aren't truly mine in this place. You're unfaithful to me with all the sounds and the smells, all the old, remembered faces; there isn't a tree that doesn't possess you . . .'

I laughed. But I did not make any reply, because I thought there was some truth in his accusation. And, besides, I no longer have my home here . . .

'We'll leave at two.'

Reassured, Renaud looked thoughtfully at the candies piled up on the table.

'Claudine, suppose we go and wake the little girls up with the sweets? What do you think?'

'Let's! Only, suppose Mademoiselle sees us . . .'

'Afraid she'll punish you with two hundred lines?'

''Course not . . . And, anyway, it'd be lots more fun if she caught us!'

'Oh, Claudine! How I love your schoolgirl soul! Come and let me bury my nose in you, you dear little reopened exercise-book.'

'Ouch! You're crumpling my covers, Renaud! . . . And Mademoiselle will be up, if we don't hurry . . .'

Laden with sweets, we walked silently along the passage, he in his blue pyjamas, I in my long, white billowing nightdress with my hair over my eyes. I listened outside the dormitory door before going in . . . Not a sound. They were as silent as little corpses. I opened the door very softly . . .

How *could* those wretched little girls sleep in broad daylight, with the sun blazing through the white curtains!

Promptly, I searched round for Hélène's bed: her charming little face was buried in the pillow and all one could see was her black plait, like an uncoiled serpent. Next to her, her little sister Isabelle lay flat on her back, her long lashes on her cheeks, wearing a virtuous, absorbed expression. Further on, the red-headed kid, sprawled like a dropped puppet, an arm here, an arm there, her mouth open and her red mop standing out like a halo, was snoring gently . . . But Renaud was staring chiefly at Pomme, Pomme who had been too hot, and was curled up like a dog on the outside of her bed, muffled in her long-sleeved nightdress, her head level with her knees and her charming little round behind thrust out . . . She had plaited her hair in a tight rope and plastered it smooth like a Chinese girl's; she had one pink cheek and one red one and her mouth and her fists were closed.

They were a charming sight, all of them! The standard of looks in the School had definitely gone up! In my time, the boarders would have inspired chastity even in that notorious 'fumbler', Dutertre . . .

Finding them as attractive as I did, and in another way too, Renaud went up close to Pomme's bed – she was quite definitely his favourite – and dropped a large green pistachio fondant on her smooth cheek. The cheek quivered, the hands opened and the charming little muffled behind shifted.

'Good morning, Pomme.'

The red-brown eyes opened roundly in startled welcome. Pomme sat up, still dazed. But her hand clapped down on the harsh green sweet. Pomme said 'Oh!' swallowed it down like a cherry and exclaimed:

'Good morning, Monsieur.'

30

At the sound of her clear voice and my laugh, the sheets on Hélène's bed rippled, the tail of the uncoiled serpent swished, and, darker than a blackcap, Hélène suddenly sat up. Sleep was difficult to shake off; she stared at us, trying to connect up today's thoughts with yesterday's; then her amber cheeks turned pink. Dishevelled and charming, she pushed back a big, obstinate lock that fell across her little nose. Then she had a good view of Pomme, sitting up, with her mouth full.

'Ah!' she squeaked in turn. 'She'll go and eat the lot.' Her squeal, her outstretched arm, and her childish anguish enchanted me. I went and squatted cross-legged on the foot of her bed, which made her draw her feet up under her and blush still more.

Her sister yawned, mumbled and put up modest hands to where the ample nightdress had come a little unbuttoned. And the carrot-headed kid, Nana, moaned covetously at the far end of the room, twisting her arms with longing . . . for Pomme, conscientious and indefatigable, was eating more and still more sweets.

'Renaud, it's cruel! Pomme is a bundle of charms, I don't deny it, but do give Hélène and the others some sweets too!'

Solemnly, he nodded his head and moved away.

'Right! Now, listen to me, all of you! I'm not giving anybody one single more sweet' . . . (palpitating silence) . . . 'unless she comes and gets it.'

They looked at each other in consternation. But little Nana had already thrust her stocky little legs out of bed and was examining her feet to see if they were clean enough to be presentable. Swiftly, holding up her long nightdress so as not to stumble, she ran up to Renaud on her bare feet that went flic, flac, on the wooden floor. With her tousled head, she looked like a child on a Christmas card. Then, catching tight hold of the full bag Renaud threw her, she went back to her bed like a contented dog.

Pomme could stand it no longer and sprang out of bed in turn. Heedless of a plump calf, gilded for a second by the sun, she ran to Renaud, who held the coveted fondants high above her head:

'Oh,' she wept, too little to reach them. '*Please*, Monsieur!'

31

And then, since this had been successful last night, she flung her arms round Renaud's neck and kissed him. It was highly successful today as well. This game was beginning to irritate me . . .

'Go on, Hélène,' muttered Isabelle, furious.

'Go on, yourself! You're the bigger. *And* the greedier too.'

'That's not true!'

'Oh, it isn't true, isn't it? All right, then. I'm not going. Pomme will eat the lot . . . I jolly well wish she'd be sick, just to teach her . . .'

At the thought of Pomme eating the lot, Isabelle jumped to the floor while I held Hélène back by her slim ankle, through the sheet.

'Don't go, Hélène. *I'll* give you some.'

Isabelle returned triumphantly. But, as she was hurriedly climbing back into her bed, the shrill voice of Nana was heard yapping:

'Isabelle's got hair on her legs! Her legs are all over hair!'

'Indecent little beast!' cried the accused. By now she was huddled up under the sheets, leaving only her shining, angry eyes visible. She reviled and threatened Nana, then her voice turned hoarse and she collapsed on her bolster in tears.

'There, Renaud! Now look what you've done!'

He laughed so loud, the mischievous fiend, that he dropped the last paperbag on the floor and it burst.

'I'll pick them up for you. What can I put them into?' I asked my little Hélène.

'I don't know. I haven't anything here – ah, I know, my basin, the third one on the wash-stand . . .'

I put all those multicoloured horrors into the enamel basin and took it over to her.

'Renaud, do just look out into the passage. Didn't I hear footsteps?'

And I remained seated on my little Hélène's bed while she sucked and nibbled and glanced at me stealthily. When I smiled at her, she promptly blushed, then plucked up courage and smiled back. She had a moist, white smile that looked fresh and appetizing.

'What are you laughing at, Hélène?'

'I'm looking at your nightdress. You look a bit like a boarder, only it's linen – no, batiste, isn't it? – and you can see through it.'

'But I am a boarder! Don't you believe me?'

'No, of course not . . . but it's such a pity you aren't.'

Things were going well. I moved closer.

'Do you like me?'

'Yes . . . awfully,' she whispered. It sounded like a sigh.

'Will you kiss me?'

'No,' she protested fiercely, in a very low, almost frightened voice.

I leant forward very close and said:

'No? I know those *noes* that mean *yes*. I've said them myself in the old days . . .'

Her imploring eyes indicated the other girls. But I felt so mischievous and so curious! And I was just going to tease her again, at even closer quarters . . . when the door opened and Renaud entered, followed by Mademoiselle in a dressing-gown. Whatever am I saying? In a house-coat, with her hair already done to face the public gaze.

'Well, Madame Claudine, do you find the boarders tempting?'

'I must say there'd be some excuse for being tempted this year.'

'Only *this* year? How marriage has altered my Claudine! . . . Come along, young ladies, do you know it's nearly eight o'clock. At a quarter to nine, I shall look under the beds, and, if I find the least thing, I shall make you sweep it up with your tongues!'

We left the dormitory with her.

'Mademoiselle, will you forgive us for this double invasion at this hour of the morning?'

Amiable and ambiguous, she answered in a low voice:

'Oh, well, in the holidays! And, as for your husband, I like to see it as a charming piece of indulgence, entirely paternal.'

I shall not forgive her for that word.

I remember the walk before lunch, the pilgrimage I wanted to make to the threshold of 'my' house of the old days which that hateful sojourn in Paris had made dearer to me than ever.

I remember the clutch at my heart that kept me standing motionless before the double flight of steps with their blackened iron railings that led to the front door. I stared fixedly at the worn copper ring I used to tug at to peal the bell when I came home from School; I stared at it so hard that I could feel it in my hand. And, as Renaud was gazing at the window of my bedroom, I looked up at him with eyes misty with tears.

'Let's go away. I can't bear it . . .'

Overcome by my misery, he led me away in silence, my arm clutched tight against his. In my mind, I turned the knob of the ground-floor window shutter with my finger – I could not stop myself . . . and it was over.

It was over, and now I regretted having wanted to come back to Montigny, impelled by regrets, love, and pride. Yes, by pride as well. I had wanted to show off my husband . . . Was he really a husband, this paternal lover, this sensual protector? . . . I had wanted to cock a snook at Mademoiselle and at her absent Aimée . . . And then – *that* would teach me – look at me now, nothing but an anguished little girl, no longer sure where I really belonged, my heart prostrate between two homes!

Entirely owing to me, lunch was a thoroughly uncomfortable meal. Mademoiselle could not make out why I looked so distressed (neither could I); the little girls, sickened with sugary stuff, could not eat. Renaud was the only one who laughed, as he teased Pomme with questions.

'Do you say yes to everything you're asked, Pomme?'

'Yes, Monsieur.'

'Pomme, I certainly don't pity the lucky man who will seek your favours, you round, pink apple. I foresee the happiest possible future for you, a future made up of fair shares for all and no quarrelling.'

Then he glanced at Mademoiselle in case she might be annoyed, but she shrugged her shoulders and said, in reply to his look:

'Oh, it doesn't matter what you say to her, she never understands.'

'Perhaps a practical demonstration would help?'

34

'You wouldn't have time before your train. Pomme never grasps anything till it's been explained four times, at the very least.'

I made a sign to stop the outrageous thing my wicked wretch of a husband was going to retort; my little Hélène, who was listening with all her ears, was already on the alert for it. ('My little Hélène' was the name I had privately given her from the first.)

Good-bye to all that! For, while I was strapping up the suitcase, there was a clatter in the courtyard, punctuated by old Racalin's oaths. Good-bye!

I had loved – and still loved – those echoing white corridors, that barracks with the pink-brick corners; I had loved the aversion inspired in me by Mademoiselle; I had loved her little Aimée, and Luce, who had never known that I did.

I stopped for a moment on that landing, with my hand on the cool wall.

Renaud, down below, beneath my feet, was having a private conversation (yet another!) with Pomme.

'Good-bye, Pomme.'

'Good-bye, Monsieur.'

'Will you write to me, Pomme?'

'I don't know your name.'

'The excuse won't hold water. I'm called "Claudine's Husband". At least, you'll be sorry to see me go?'

'Yes, Monsieur.'

'Especially on account of the sweets?'

'Oh, yes, Monsieur!'

'Pomme, your shameless candour inspires me with enthusiasm. Kiss me!'

Behind me, something rustled very softly . . . My little Hélène was there. I turned round; she stood there, pretty and silent, a study in black and white; I smiled at her. She wanted very much to say something to me. But I knew it was too difficult and she could only gaze at me with lovely black-and-white eyes. Then as, down below, Pomme clasped herself round Renaud's neck with placid docility, I put one arm round this silent little girl who smelt of cedar-wood pencils

35

and sandalwood fans. It was on her resilient mouth that I said good-bye to my youthful past . . .

To my youthful past? . . . Here, at least, I might as well not lie . . . Hélène, trembling and already passionate as she ran to the window to watch me go, you will never know something that would surprise and hurt you: what I kissed on your clinging, inexpert mouth was only the ghost of Luce . . .

Before talking to Renaud, in the train that carried us away, I gave one last look at the tower, hooded over by a woolly mass of thickening storm clouds; I watched it till it vanished behind the round back of a hill. Then, relieved, as if I had said good-bye to someone, I returned to my dear, frivolous man, who, so as not to break the habit, was saying admiring things and holding me close and . . . but I interrupted him.

'Tell me, Renaud, is it awfully nice, kissing that Pomme?'

I looked earnestly into his eyes, without being able to see into the blue-black depths of them; it was like looking into a bottomless lake.

'That Pomme? Darling, you wouldn't be doing me the great honour of being jealous? Nothing would give me more intense pleasure!'

'Oh, don't think it's an honour! Pomme isn't my idea of an honourable victory.'

'My slenderest, loveliest of girls, if you'd said: "Don't kiss Pomme!" it wouldn't even have been any merit for me to have kept off her!'

Yes. He would do whatever I wanted. But he had not given a straight answer to my question: 'Is it awfully nice, kissing that Pomme?' He is adept at never giving himself away, at sliding out of things, at smoothing me with evasive tenderness.

He loves me, there is no doubt whatever of that, more than anything in the world. Thank God, I love him – that is certain too. But how much more feminine he is than I am! How much simpler I feel I am, how much more ruthless . . . more sombre . . . more passionate.

I expressly avoid saying: more upright. I could have said it a year and some months ago. At that time, I would not have given in so quickly to temptation, up there on the dormitory landing. I would not have kissed that young mouth, cold and moist as a split fruit, under the pretence of saying good-bye to my schoolgirl past, to my black-overalled childhood self. I would only have kissed the desk over which Luce had bent her stubborn brow.

For a year and a half, I have been aware of the progress of the slow and pleasant corruption within myself that I owe to Renaud. When one looks at them through his eyes, big things grow small and all that is serious in life is reduced to triviality. On the other hand, futile trivialities, especially if they are harmful, assume an enormous importance. But how can I defend myself against the incurable and engaging frivolity that prevails over everything else in him and sweeps me along in his wake?

There is something worse: through Renaud I have discovered the secret of giving and receiving sensual delight, and the possession and use of it gives me the thrill of a child wielding a deadly weapon. He has revealed to me the sure and urgent power of my tall, lithe, muscular body – hard buttocks, scarcely any breasts, an even-textured skin as smooth as porcelain – of my Egyptian tobacco eyes that have grown deeper and more restless, of a short, bushy mane the colour of ripening chestnuts . . . All this new strength I exert, only half-consciously, on Renaud – just as, had I stayed two days more at the school, I should have exerted it on that charming Hélène.

Yes, yes, I admit it, but do not press me further. Otherwise I shall say that Renaud was responsible for my kissing my little Hélène on the lips.

THREE

'SMALL AND SILENT Claudine, what are you thinking about?' He asked me that, I remember, on the hotel terrace at Heidelberg, while my eyes were wandering from the ample curve of the Neckar to the sham ruins of the Schloss down below us.

Sitting on the ground, I raised my chin from the props of my two fists.

'I'm thinking of the garden.'

'What garden?'

'Oh, "What garden"! The garden at Montigny, of course!'

Renaud threw away his cigarette. He lives, like a god, in clouds of fragrant Egyptian tobacco smoke.

'Funny little girl . . . With *that* landscape in front of you! Are you going to tell me it's more beautiful than this, the garden at Montigny?'

'Of course not. But it's mine.'

That was just it! Over and over again we had discussed it, but neither could understand the other. Renaud would kiss me affectionately, a little contemptuously, and call me a lazy little stay-at-home and a gipsy who wouldn't leave her tent. I would laugh and retort that *his* home was in a suitcase. We were both right, but I blamed him because he did not think as I did.

He has travelled too much and I not enough. There is nothing nomadic about me, except my mind. I cheerfully follow Renaud in his wanderings because I adore him. But I like journeys that have an end. He is in love with travel for travel's sake; he gets up happily under a foreign sky, thinking that today he will be off somewhere else. He longs for the mountains of one nearby country, for the harsh wine of another, for the artificial charm of this dolled-up watering-place ablaze with flowers, for the solitude of that high-perched hamlet. And he goes off, with no regrets for the hamlet or the flowers or the potent wine.

I follow him. And I enjoy – yes, truly I enjoy them too – the friendly town, the sun behind the pine-trees, the echoing mountain air. But round my ankle I feel a thread whose other end is wound and knotted round the old walnut-tree in the garden at Montigny.

I don't think I am an unnatural daughter! And yet there is something I have to admit: I have missed Fanchette during our travels almost as much as Papa. The only time I really missed my noble father badly was in Germany, where those Wagnerian chromolithographs and picture-postcards reminded me of him. All the representations of Odin and Wotan, apart from the missing eye, resembled him. Like him, they were handsome, they brandished harmless thunderbolts and they displayed tempestuous beards and commanding gestures. And I could imagine that, like his, their vocabulary included all the coarse expressions of a mythical bygone age.

I wrote to him seldom and he rarely replied. His letters were affectionate and higgledy-piggledy, written in a juicily hybrid style, in which periods whose cadence would have delighted Chateaubriand (I am flattering Papa a little) harboured in their bosom – their august bosom – the most scarifying oaths. I learnt from these anything but commonplace letters that, apart from the silent, faithful Monsieur Maria, who was still the perfect secretary, nothing was going right . . . 'I don't know whether to blame your absence for it, little donkey,' my dear father confided to me, 'but I'm beginning to find Paris pestilential, especially since that specimen of the dregs of humanity by name of X . . . has just published a treatise on *Universal Malacology* stupid enough to make even the squatting lions outside the Institute vomit. How can the Eternal Justice still pour forth the light of the day on such filthy skunks?

Mélie wrote to me also, well describing Fanchette's state of mind since my departure; how she had wailed in desolation for days and days. But Mélie's handwriting is so hieroglyphic that it is impossible to keep up a sustained correspondence with her.

Fanchette was mourning me! The thought of this haunted me wherever I went. All the time I was on my travels, I started at the sight of every lean tomcat fleeing round the corner of a wall. Over and over again, to Renaud's surprise, I have let go his arm to run up to a she-cat, sitting sedately on a doorstep, and say to her: 'My Sweeeet!' Often the little animal would be shocked and tuck in her chin, with a dignified movement, against her ruffled shirt-front. But I would insist, adding a series of shrill onomatopoeic noises in a minor key until I saw the green eyes melt into gentleness and narrow in smile. Then the flat, caressing head would rub hard against the door-post in polite greeting and the cat would turn round three times, which clearly meant: 'I like you.'

Never once did Renaud show any impatience during these bouts of cat-mania. But I suspect him of being more indulgent than understanding. He is quite capable, monster that he is, of never having stroked my Fanchette except out of diplomacy.

How willingly I look back over this recent past and dwell on it! But Renaud lives in the future. This paradoxical man who is devoured by the terror of growing old, who studies himself minutely in looking-glasses and desperately notes every tiny wrinkle in the network at the corner of his eyes, is uneasy in the present and feverishly hurries Today on Tomorrow. I myself linger in the past, even if that past be only Yesterday, and I look back almost always with regret. It is as if marriage (be honest and say sex!) had developed certain modes of 'feeling' in me that were older than myself. This amazes Renaud. But he loves me, and if, as my lover, he no longer understands me, I can still take refuge in the other Renaud, my dear, great fatherly friend! For him, I am a trusting daughter who leans on her self-chosen father and confides in him, almost without the lover's knowledge. Better still, if Renaud-the-lover tries to insinuate himself as a third between Papa-Renaud and Daughter-Claudine, the latter gives him a ruthless reception. She pushes him away like a cat who's jumped up on one's desk. So then the poor thing has to wait, impatient and disappointed, until the other Claudine returns, light-hearted and rested, to bring him her swiftly overcome resistance, her silence and her fire.

Alas, all I have put down here, more or less at random, does not make me see where the rift between us lies. Nevertheless, how conscious, how terribly conscious, of it I am!

Here we are, in our own place at last! All the tiring shopping expeditions of our return are over; Renaud's fevered anxiety that I should like my new home has calmed down.

He begged me to choose between two flats, both of which are his. (Two flats; that's none too many for one Renaud . . .) 'If you don't fancy them, darling child, we'll find another one that's prettier than these two.' I resisted the desire to reply: 'Show me the third one,' and, overcome once more by my insurmountable horror of moving, I examined the two quite conscientiously; above all, I had a good sniff at them. And, finding the smell of this one more sympathetic to my hypersensitive nose, I chose it. It needed very little more in the way of furniture, but Renaud, scrupulous over details and much more feminine and houseproud than myself, used all his ingenuity ferreting round for objects to complete a flawless whole. Anxious to please me, anxious too not to include anything that might offend his over-critical eye, he consulted me twenty times over. My first answer was sincere: 'It's all the same to me!' My second too. But on the subject of the bed, 'that keystone of conjugal bliss', to use Papa's expression, I gave my opinion very definitely.

'I'd like my little four-poster with the chintz curtains.'

At which my poor Renaud flung up his arms in despair.

'Misery me! A four-poster in a Louis XV bedroom! Besides, my darling, monstrous little girl, do use your imagination! We should have to add an extension to lengthen it . . . I mean, widen it . . .'

Yes, I realized that only too well. But what could you expect? I couldn't feel much interest in furniture that I didn't know – not yet. The big low bed has become my friend, and so have the dressing-room and a few vast padded armchairs. But the rest continues to regard me, if I dare use the expression, with a mistrustful eye; the wardrobe with the long mirror squints at me when I pass, the drawing-room table with its curved legs tries to trip me up and I kick it back good and hard.

Two months, Lord, two months – isn't that long enough to break in a flat? And I stifle the voice of reason that growls: 'In two months, you can tame plenty of pieces of furniture, but not one Claudine.'

Would Fanchette consent to live here? I saw her again at Papa's flat in the rue Jacob, my darling white beautiful. She had not been warned of my return and it made my heart heavy to see her prostrate with emotion at my feet, unable to utter a sound, while, with my hand on her warm pink stomach, I tried vainly to count the wild pulsations of her heart. I laid her on her side to comb her dulled coat; at that familiar gesture, she raised her head with a look full of so many things – reproach, unfailing love, torment accepted with joy . . . Oh, little white animal, how close I feel to you because I understand you so well!

I have seen my noble father again, tall and broad with his tricoloured beard, brimming over with sonorous words and ineffective pugnacity. Without being consciously aware of it, we love each other and I understand all the genuine pleasure implied by his first words of welcome: 'Would you deign to give me a kiss, you vile slut?' I think he has grown larger in the last two years. I'm not joking! And the proof is that he confessed to me that he felt cramped in the rue Jacob. I admit that he did add afterwards: 'You know, this last year or two, I've been picking up books, for nothing, in the sale-rooms. Nineteen hundred at least . . . A thousand herds of sacred swine! I've been forced to stuff them away in the box-room! It's so small, this pig-sty . . . Whereas, in that room at the back at Montigny, I could . . .' He turned away his head and pulled his beard, but our eyes had had time to meet and exchange an odd look. He's b . . . well, I mean he's *quite* capable of going back there just as he came here, for no reason at all . . .

I am avoiding the thing that is painful to me to write.

Perhaps it isn't in the least serious? If only it weren't in the least serious! Here it is:

Since yesterday, everything has been in place in Ren . . . in our flat. We shall see no more of the fussy niggling of the carpet-layer nor of the incurable absentmindedness of the curtain-hanger, who, every five minutes, kept mislaying his little brass gadgets for a quarter of an hour. Renaud feels at ease, and wanders about smiling approval at a clock that is right, bullying a picture that is not hanging straight. He tucked me under his arm to take me round on our proprietorial tour, then left me (no doubt to go off and do his work on the *Diplomatic Review*, to settle the fate of Europe with Jacobsen and treat Abdul Hamid as he deserved), alone in the drawing-room. He left me, after a satisfying kiss, saying: 'My little despot, your kingdom is yours to rule.'

Sitting there, with nothing to do, I drifted off into a long day-dream. Then an hour struck – I have no idea which – and brought me to my feet, quite unaware that I was living in the present. The next thing I knew, I was standing in front of the glass over the chimneypiece, hurriedly pinning on my hat . . . *to go home*.

That was all. But it was a shattering experience. It conveys nothing to *you*? You're lucky.

To go home! But where? Isn't this my own home, then? No, no, it isn't, and that's the whole source of my trouble. To go home? Where? Definitely not to the rue Jacob, where Papa has piled up mountains of papers on my bed. Not to Montigny, because neither the beloved house . . . nor the School . . .

To go home! Have I no real dwelling then? No! I live here with a man, admittedly a man I love, but I am living with a man! Alas, Claudine, plant torn up from its soil, did your roots go as deep as all that? What will Renaud say? Nothing. He can do nothing.

Where would I find a burrow? Within myself. I must dig into my misery, into my irrational, indescribable misery, and curl myself up in that hole.

I sat down again and, with my hat still on my head and my hands clenched tight together, I burrowed.

43

My diary has no future. It is five months now since I abandoned it on an unhappy note, and I feel resentful towards it. In any case, I haven't time to keep it up to date. Renaud is taking me about and exhibiting me in the social world – almost every variety of it – far more than I like. But since he's proud of me, I can't hurt him by refusing to accompany him . . .

His marriage – I hadn't realized this – has made a great stir among the variegated (I nearly wrote 'motley') crowd of people he knows. No, he doesn't know them. He himself is tremendously well known. But he's incapable of putting a name to half the individuals with whom he exchanges cordial handshakes and whom he introduces to me. Frittering himself away, incorrigibly frivolous, he is not seriously attached to anything – except to me. 'Who's that man, Renaud?' 'It's . . . Bother, I can't remember his name.' Well! Apparently, his profession demands this sort of thing; apparently the fact of writing profound articles for serious diplomatic journals infallibly necessitates your shaking hands with a horde of affected people, including painted women (of the world and the half-world), clinging and pushing 'actresses', painters and models . . .

But Renaud puts so much husbandly and fatherly pride (the ingenuous tenderness of it touches me, coming from this blasé Parisian) into those three words, 'My wife, Claudine', that I draw in my claws and smooth out the angry creases between my eyebrows. And, besides, I have other compensations: a revengeful pleasure in answering, when Renaud vaguely points out to me a 'Monsieur . . . Durande':

'You told me the day before yesterday that his name was Dupont!'

'Did I tell you that? Are you sure? I've mixed them both up with . . . well, the other one. That moron who calls me "Old Boy" because we were in the Sixth together.'

All the same, I find it hard to get used to such nebulous intimacies.

Here and there, in the lobbies of the Opéra-Comique, at Chevillard and Colonne concerts, at soirées, particularly at soirées – at the moment when the fear of music casts a gloom over faces – I have overheard remarks about myself that were not entirely benevolent. So people are gossiping about me? Ah! of course, here I am Renaud's wife, just as, in Montigny, he is Claudine's husband. These Parisians speak low, but people who come from Fresnois can hear the grass grow.

They say: 'She's very young.' They say: 'Too dark . . . she looks bad-tempered . . .' 'What, too dark? she's got chestnut curls—' 'That short hair, it's to attract attention! All the same, Renaud has taste.' They say: 'Where on earth does she come from? . . . She's from Montmartre . . . It's Slavonic, that small chin and broad temples. She's straight out of one of Pierre Loüys's homosexual novels.' . . . 'Surely it's a bit early to have got to the stage of only liking little girls. How old *is* Renaud?'

Renaud, always Renaud . . . Here is something characteristic: No one ever refers to him except by his first name.

FOUR

YESTERDAY MY HUSBAND asked me:

'Claudine, will you have an at-home day?'

'Heavens above, whatever for?'

'To gossip, to "argle-bargle" as you say.'

'With whom?'

'With women of the world.'

'I don't much like women of the world.'

'With men too.'

'Don't tempt me! . . . No, I won't have an at-home day. Do you imagine I know how to be a society hostess?'

'*I* have one, you know!'

'You *do*? . . . All right, keep it: I'll come and visit you on your at-home day. Honestly, it's much less risky. Otherwise, after an hour I'm quite likely to say to your gorgeous lady friends: "Get out. I'm fed up with you. You make me sick."'

He did not insist (he never insists); he kissed me (he always kisses me) and went out of the room, laughing.

My stepson, Marcel, overwhelms me with polite contempt for this misanthropy and this frightened dislike of the 'world' I am always proclaiming. That little boy, so completely unsusceptible to women, assiduously seeks their company; he gossips, fingers materials, pours out tea without staining delicate dresses, and adores talking scandal. I am wrong in calling him 'that little boy'. At twenty, one is no longer a little boy and *he* will remain a little girl for a long time. On my return to Paris, I found him still charming, but all the same a little worm. He is excessively thin now, his eyes are bigger and

46

have a wild, strained look and there are three premature fine wrinkles at the corner of the lids . . . Is Charlie the only one responsible for them?

Renaud's anger against this two-faced little cheat did not last very long. 'I can't forget that he's my child, Claudine. And perhaps, if I'd brought him up better . . .' I myself forgave Marcel out of indifference. (Indifference, pride, and an unadmitted – and rather low-down – interest in the aberrations of his love-life.) And I feel a keen pleasure that never loses its edge every time I look under the left eye of that boy who ought to have been a girl and see the white line left by my scratch!

But that Marcel amazes me! I had been expecting implacable resentment and open hostility. Not a trace of anything of the kind! Irony frequently, disdain too, curiosity – and that's all.

His one and only preoccupation is himself! He is constantly gazing into mirrors, putting his two forefingers on his eyebrows and pushing up the skin of his forehead as high as it will go. Surprised by this gesture, which is becoming a morbid habit, I asked him the meaning of it. 'It's to rest the skin under the eyes,' he replied with the utmost seriousness. He lengthens the curve of his eyelids with a blue pencil; he risks wearing over-ornamental turquoise cuff-links. Ugh! At forty, he will be sinister . . .

In spite of what happened between us, he feels no embarrassment at making me partial confidences, either out of unconscious bravado or as a result of his increasing moral perversion. He was here yesterday, languishing the tired charm of his too-slender body and his brilliant, fevered eyes.

'You look utterly exhausted, Marcel!'

'I *am* utterly exhausted.'

We always adopt an aggressive tone with each other. It's a kind of game and means very little.

'Charlie again?'

'Oh, for goodness' sake! . . . A young woman oughtn't to know about certain disorders of the mind. Or, if she does, she ought to have the decency to forget them. 'Disorders" *is* what you call them, isn't it?'

'"Disorders" is certainly what they're called . . . But I would hardly say "of the mind".'

'Thanks for the body. But, between you and me, my tiredness has nothing whatever to do with Charlie, so he needn't flatter himself it has. Charlie! A waverer, neither one thing nor the other . . .'

'I say, come now!'

'Believe me. I know him better than you do . . .'

'So I should hope! Thanks for the compliment.'

'Yes, at bottom he's a coward.'

'When you really get to the bottom . . .'

'It's ancient history, our friendship. I'm not repudiating it; I'm breaking it. And because of some not very savoury incidents . . .'

'What, the beautiful Charlie? Has he been twisting you over money?'

'Worse than that. He accidentally left a wallet behind at my place – full of women's letters!'

With what hatred and disgust he spat out his accusation! I stared at him, profoundly thoughtful. He was a pervert, an unfortunate – almost irresponsible – child, but his fury was justified. One had only to put oneself in his place in imagination. Yes, I should have felt the same.

It is laid down that everything – joys, sorrows, trivial events – should come upon me suddenly. Not, goodness knows, that I go in for the extraordinary . . . apart from one exception – my marriage. But time goes by for me like the big hand of certain public clocks; it stays perfectly still where it is for fifty-nine seconds, then all at once, with no transition, it jumps to the next minute with a spasmodic jerk. The minutes grab it roughly as they do me . . . I am not saying that is entirely and invariably unpleasant, but . . .

My last jump was this: I went to see Papa, Mélie, Fanchette, and Limaçon. This last, striped and splendid, fornicates with his mother and takes us back to the worst days of the House of Atreus. The rest of the time, he prowls about the flat, arrogant, leonine, and fierce. Not one of the virtues of his lovable white mother has been passed down to him.

Mélie rushed to meet me, holding the globe of her left

breast in her hand, like Charlemagne holding the terrestrial orb.

'My darling, precious lamb . . . I was just going to drop you a line! If you knew the state we're in here. All upside-down, you'd think the end of the world was come. I say, aren't you fetching in that hat? . . .'

'Pipe down, pipe down! So the end of the world's come! Why? Has Limaçon overturned his . . . spittoon?'

Wounded by my sarcasm, Mélie withdrew.

'You think I'm joking? All right, go and ask Monsieur – you'll see with your very own eyes.'

Intrigued, I walked into Papa's study without knocking. He turned round when he heard me, unmasking an enormous packing case that he was filling with books. His handsome, hirsute face wore an entirely new expression; harmless rage, embarrassment, childish confusion.

'Is that you, little donkey?'

'It would seem so. What on earth are you doing, Papa?'

'I . . . I'm putting some papers in order.'

'Funny kind of file you've got there! But – I know that packing case . . . That comes from Montigny, that does!'

Papa resigned himself to the inevitable. He buttoned up his tight-waisted frock-coat, sat down, taking his time about it, and crossed his arms over his beard.

'That comes from Montigny and that is going back there! Do I make myself clear?'

'No, not in the least.'

He stared at me under his bushy, beetling eyebrows, lowered his voice and risked coming right out with it:

'I'm buggering off!'

I had understood perfectly well. I had felt that this irrational flight was coming. Why had he come? Why was he going away? Idle to ask. Papa is a force of Nature; he serves the obscure designs of Fate. Without knowing it, he came here in order that I might meet Renaud; he is going away, having fulfilled his mission of irresponsible father.

As I had made no answer, that terrible man recovered his self-confidence.

'You realize, I've had enough of it! I'm ruining my eyes in

49

this pitch-dark hole. I'm surrounded by rogues and scoundrels and bunglers. I can't stir a finger without banging against a wall, the wings of my spirit are broken with beating against universal ignorance. A thousand herds of abysmal, mangy swine! I'm going back to my old hovel. Will you come and see me there with that highwayman you married?'

That Renaud! He has captivated even Papa, who rarely sees him, but never speaks of him except in a special tone of gruff affection.

'You bet I'll come.'

'But . . . I've got all sorts of important things to say to you. What's to be done with the cat? She's used to me, that animal . . .'

'The cat?'

The cat! It's true . . . he's very fond of her. Besides, Mélie would be there, and I feel apprehensive for Fanchette when I think of Renaud's manservant and Renaud's cook . . . My darling, my sweet girl, nowadays I sleep beside a warm body that is not yours . . . I made up my mind.

'Take her with you. Later on, I'll see; perhaps I'll have her back with me.'

But what I was most conscious of was that, on the pretext of filial duty, I would be able to see the house of enchanted memories again, just as I had left it, revisit the dear and dubious School . . . In my heart, I blessed my father's exodus.

'Take my bedroom with you too, Papa. I'll sleep in it when we come to see you.'

With one gesture, the bulwark of Malacology crushed me to powder with his contempt.

'Ugh! You wouldn't blush to cohabit with your husband under my unpolluted roof, impure animals as all you females are! What does it mean to you, the regenerating power of chastity?'

How I love him when he's like that! I kissed him and went away, leaving him burying his treasures in the vast packing-case and gaily humming a folk-song he adores:

There was a young maiden as I have heard tell,
And the language of flowers she knew passing well;

50

She would finger and fondle her sweet Shepherd's Purse:
You can all take my meaning for better or worse.

A hymn, presumably, to regenerating Chastity!

'Definitely, darling, I'm going to start having my day again.'

Renaud broke this grave news to me in our dressing-room
where I was taking off my clothes. We had spent the evening
at old Madame Barmann's and assisted, by way of a change,
at a good old squabble between that fat female screech-owl
and the noisy boor who shares her destiny. She said to him:
'You're common!' He retorted: 'You bore everyone to tears
with your literary pretensions!' He bellowed; she screeched.
The altercation continued. Running out of invectives, he flung
down his napkin, left the table and stormed upstairs to his
room. Everybody sighed and relaxed and we went on with
our dinner in peace. When we reached the sweet course, our
amiable hostess dispatched her personal maid, Eugénie, to
soothe the fat man down (by what mysterious process?) and
he finally came downstairs again, calmed, but offering not the
slightest apology. However, Gréveuille, the exquisite member
of the Academy, who is terrified of rows, laid the blame on his
venerable mistress, flattered the husband, and helped himself
to some more cheese.

My own personal contribution to this charming milieu
consists of my curly head, my soft, suspicious eyes, the
discrepancy between my full, firm neck and my thin shoulders
revealed by my *décolletage*, and a mutism that embarrasses
my neighbours at dinner.

The men do not make up to me. My recent marriage still
keeps them at a distance and I am not the kind of female who
tries to attract flirtatious admirers.

One Wednesday, at that old Barmann woman's, I was
politely pursued by a young and attractive literary man.
(Beautiful eyes that boy, a faint touch of blepharitis, but no
matter . . .) He compared me – my short hair as usual! – to
Myrtocleia, to a young Hermes, to an Eros by Prud'hon – he
raked his memories of private art collections for me and cited
so many hermaphroditic masterpieces that I began to think of

Luce and Marcel and he nearly ruined a marvellous dish for me. It was a heavenly *cassoulet*, a speciality of the Barmann's cook, served in little silver-handled *cocottes*. 'Such an advantage having one's own *cocotte*, isn't it? *Cher Maître?* One can be sure of getting enough to eat,' whispered Maugis in Gréveuille's ear, and the sixty-year-old sponger, who was the hostess's lover, agreed with a one-sided smile.

After dinner, the little flatterer, excited by his own evocations, would not leave me alone. Huddled up in a Louis XV armchair, I could hear him, though I was hardly listening, going on with his endless literary comparisons. He gazed at me with his caressing, long-lashed eyes, and murmured so that the others could not hear:

'Ah, your dreaming is the dreaming of the boy Narcissus, your soul, like his, is full of bitterness and sensuous delight.'

'Monsieur,' I told him firmly, 'you are completely off the track. My soul is full of nothing but haricot beans and little strips of bacon.'

Dumbfounded, he said no more.

Renaud scolded me a little and laughed a great deal.

'You're going to start having your day again, dear Renaud?'

He had ensconced his large body in a wicker armchair and I was undressing with my usual chaste unselfconsciousness. Chaste? Let us say, innocent of any ulterior motive.

'Yes. What do you intend to do, my darling child? You looked very pretty and very wan just now at the hook-nosed Barmann's.'

'What do I intend to do when you start your day again? Why, I intend to go and see you.'

'Is that all?' said his disappointed chin.

'Yes, that's all. It's *your* day, isn't it? How else do I come into it?'

'But, hang it all, Claudine, you're my wife!'

'And whose fault is that? If you'd listened to me, I'd be your mistress, tucked away all nice and quiet in a little hideout, somewhere, miles away from all your social world. Then your receptions could go on in their old normal way. I do wish you'd behave as if you were my lover . . .'

Good heavens, he took me at my word! Because I had just picked up my mauve silk petticoat from the floor with an agile foot, my big husband advanced on me, excited by the double Claudine reflected in the glass.

'Get away from me, Renaud! That gentleman in evening dress, that little girl in her knickers, no really! It's like a scene out of Marcel Prévost . . . when he's looking licentious in a big way . . .'

The truth is, Renaud likes tell-tale mirrors and their bright, lewd connivance, whereas I fly from them, disdaining their revelations, instinctively seeking darkness, silence, and blind ecstasy . . .

'Renaud, you wretch! We were talking about your day.'

'To blazes with my day! I prefer your night!'

FIVE

SO PAPA HAS gone away exactly as he came. I did not accompany him to the station, having little desire to witness his tempestuous departure. I did not need to be there to know what it would be like. Wrapped in a storm-cloud, he would rage against the 'filthy rabble' of railway employees, shower them contemptuously with sumptuous tips, and forget to pay for his ticket.

Mélie is sincerely sorry to leave me but 'at moment', the permission to take Fanchette with her will be staunching all her regrets. Poor Mélie, her *lammy* remains incomprehensible to her! What, I've married the man of my choice; what, I sleep with him as much as I want to – and even more – I live in a pretty *höam*, I have a manservant, a carriage hired by the month – and I don't put on any more swank? Mélie thinks I ought to go about positively flaunting my good fortune.

I wonder . . . is there possibly a grain of truth in her criticism? In Renaud's presence I don't think of anything except him. He is more engrossing than a petted woman. His intense vitality manifests itself in smiles, in words, in constant humming, in amorous demands; tenderly, he accuses me of not wooing him, of being able to read in his presence, of having my eyes too often fixed on some point in space. Out of his presence, I feel the embarrassment of an abnormal, illicit situation. Am I totally unsuited to the 'estate of matrimony'?

Yet I ought to be able to get used to it. After all, Renaud has only got what he deserves. All he had to do was not to marry me . . .

54

Oyez! Oyez! My husband has resumed his at-home day.
Word has gone round.

What can Renaud have done in the sight of the Lord to
deserve so many friends? The manservant Ernest has ushered
at least forty people into the leather-upholstered study that
smells pleasantly of Turkish tobacco and the long hall to
which we banished all drawings and sketches, whoever the
artist. The crowd included men, women, and Marcel.

At the first ring of the bell, I leapt to my feet and ran and
locked myself into the comforting dressing-room. It rang – it
rang again. At every trill, the skin of my back stirred
unpleasantly and I thought of Fanchette who, on rainy days,
watches the big drops dripping from the broken gutter with
the same nervous ripples running down her spine . . . Alas, I
was all too like Fanchette! For, in a few moments, Renaud
was parleying with me through the locked door of my refuge.

'Claudine, little girl, this is becoming impossible. At first I
said you hadn't come home yet, but, I assure you, the
situation's getting critical: Maugis is insisting that I keep you
in the cellar, God only knows where . . .'

I listened to him, looking at myself in the glass and laughing
in spite of myself.

The beast! He had said the one thing that would have any
effect! I brushed my hair over my forehead and made sure my
skirt was properly done up; then I opened the door.

'Can I appear in front of your friends like this?'

'Yes, of course. I adore you in black.'

'Oh, you adore me in all colours!'

'Most of all in flesh-colour, it's true . . . Come quick!'

People had already been smoking a lot in my husband's flat;
the smell of tea hovered in the air along with that of ginger –
and those strawberries, and those ham and *foie gras* and
caviare sandwiches. How quickly a hot room begins to smell
like a restaurant!

I sat down and I 'paid a call'. My husband offered me tea,
as if I were simply the latest arrival, and it was the pretty
Cypriot with the paradoxical name, Madame van
Langendonck, who brought me cream. What luck!

Here, at . . . Renaud's, I could identify various figures I had

55

vaguely met at theatres and concerts: critics, great and small, some with their wives, some with their mistresses. That was just as it should be. I had insisted that my husband should not do any purging – horrible word! the thing itself would have been just as ugly. And, as I have said, I was not the hostess.

Maugis, with a claret glass full of Kümmel in his hand, was questioning, with marvellously simulated interest, the author of a feminist novel, who was explaining at length the theme of his next book. The novelist talked on, indefatigably: the other never stopped drinking. When he was sufficiently drunk, he finally asked in a thick voice:

'And . . . and the title of this powerful work?'

'It isn't decided yet. Not till I've polished off the book.'

'I hope you'll polish yourself off first.'

With which he moved quickly away.

Among the numerous foreigners, I picked out a Spanish sculptor with beautiful eyes, like a horse's, a clear-cut mouth, and an incomplete knowledge of our language. He was mainly interested in painting and I admitted, without embarrassment, that I hardly knew anything in the Louvre and felt no particular passion to enlighten my ignorance.

'You no know the Rubenses?'

'No.'

'You have not the wish to see them?'

'No.'

At this, he rose to his feet, 'made a leg' with Andalusian grace, and, with a deep, respectful bow, announced crushingly:

'You are a swine, Madame.'

A lovely lady who belongs to the Opéra (and to one of Renaud's men friends) gave a start and stared at us, hoping for a scene. But she wasn't going to get it. I had completely understood this Spanish aesthete, who had only one disparaging term at his disposal. He only knows the word 'swine'; in France we have only one word for the different varieties of 'love', which is every bit as ridiculous.

Someone had come in and Renaud exclaimed:

'I thought you were in London! So it's sold, then?'

'It's sold. We're living in Paris,' said a tired voice with a faint, hardly perceptible English accent.

The man was tall and fair, and held himself very upright, carrying his small head, with its brick complexion and opaque blue eyes, very straight on his square shoulders. He was, as I say, square shouldered and well built, but he had the stiffness of a man who is thinking all the time about holding himself straight and appearing robust.

His wife . . . we were introduced to each other without my really listening, I was too busy looking at her. I noticed almost at once one of the most definite sources of her charm: all her movements, the turn of her hips, the arching of her neck, the quick raising of her arm to her hair, the sway of her seated body, all described curves so nearly circular that I could see the design of interlacing rings, like the perfect spirals of sea shells, that her gentle movements left traced on the air.

Her long-lashed eyes, of a changeable amber-shot grey, looked darker under the light gold wavy hair that had a greenish tinge in it. A black velvet dress, its too sumptuous material very plainly cut, clung to her round, mobile hips and her slim but not squeezed-in waist. A tiny diamond star, the head of a long pin, glittered among the drooping feathers of her hat.

She drew a swift, hot little hand out of her fox muff and put it in mine, whilst her eyes looked me up and down. I was almost sure she was going to speak with a foreign accent. I don't know why, but, in spite of the faultless dress, the absence of jewellery – she did not even wear a necklace – she struck me as a trifle flashy. Her eyes did not look like a Frenchwoman's. She spoke . . . I pricked up my ears . . . and she spoke without the faintest trace of accent! How stupid one is to get preconceived ideas! Her fresh mouth, tight in repose, became flower-like and tempting when she opened it. She broke at once into complimentary remarks:

'I'm so delighted to meet you. I was sure your husband would unearth a little wife who would surprise and ravish us all!'

'Thank you on my husband's behalf! But now won't you pay me a compliment that doesn't flatter anyone but me?'

'You don't need one. Just resign yourself to looking unlike anyone else.'

She hardly moved and made only restrained gestures, yet, merely in the act of sitting down beside me, she seemed to swirl round twice inside her dress.

Were we already mutually attracted or hostile? No, definitely attracted: in spite of her praise just now, I felt not the slightest desire to scratch her; she was charming. From closer range, I counted her spirals and her multiple curves; her supple hair swirled on her nape, her ear traced complex and delicate whorls, while her ray-like lashes and the quivering plumes swathed round her hat seemed to be whirling round, independent of her, in invisible gyrations.

I was tempted to ask her how many spinning dervishes she numbered among her ancestors. But I knew I mustn't; Renaud would scold me. And, anyway, why be in such a hurry to shock this endearing Madame Lambrook?

'Have you heard Renaud talk about us?' she inquired.

'Never. Do you know each other very well?'

'I should think we do! . . . We must have dined together at least half a dozen times. And I'm not counting big dinner parties.'

Was she laughing at me? Was she sarcastic or silly? That was something I should find out later on. For the moment, I was enchanted by her slow speech, and her caressing voice that lingered now and then, coolingly, on a rebellious *rrr*.

I let her go on talking and, all the while, she gazed closely into my eyes with her short-sighted ones, coolly verifying their colour that matches my short hair.

And she told me about herself. In a quarter of an hour I knew that her husband was a retired British officer sapped and burnt-out by India, where he had left the last of his physical strength and his mental activity. He was nothing now but a handsome carcass – she made that very clear. I knew she was rich, but 'never anything like rich enough,' she said passionately, that her Viennese mother had given her beautiful hair, a skin like a white convolvulus (I quote), and the name of Rézi.

'Rézi . . . it sounds like a delicious fruit . . . What an unusual name!'

'In France, yes. But in Vienna I believe it's anything but

unusual. Almost as common a diminutive as Nana or Titine
here.'

'I don't care . . . Rézi. How charming it is, that name Rézi!'

'It's charming because you say it charmingly.'

Her bare fingers stroked my bare nape, so swiftly that I
started, more as a nervous reflex than in surprise. For I had
been aware, for the last two minutes, of her darting eyes
encircling my neck with a chain of glances.

'Rézi . . .'

It was her husband this time, wanting to take her away. He
had come to say good-bye to me and his opaque blue eyes
embarrassed me. A handsome carcass! I thought it might still
house a good deal of jealousy and tyranny, for, at his laconic
summons, Rézi rose at once, making no demur. That man
expresses himself in slow, spaced-out phrases (like an actor
being prompted every three words, Maugis says). Obviously,
he is careful about his diction so as to suppress all trace of
English accent.

It was agreed that 'we would see each other often' and that
'Madame Claudine was a marvel'. If I keep my promise, I
shall go and see that blonde Rézi in her flat, only two steps
away, in the Avenue Kléber.

Rézi . . . Her whole person gives off a scent of fern and
iris, a respectable, artless, rustic smell that I find surprising
and enchanting by contrast. For I can discover nothing
artless or rustic in her, least of all anything respectable, she
is far too pretty! She talked to me about her husband and
her travels, but I know nothing about herself, except her
charm . . .

'Well, Claudine . . .?'

My dear giant, worn out and happy, was contentedly
surveying the drawing-room, empty at last. Dirty plates, little
cakes nibbled at and left, dead cigarettes on the arms of chairs
and the edges of tables (have they no shame, these beastly
visitors?), glasses sticky with appalling mixtures of drinks. I
had caught a classically hirsute poet from Provence busy
combining orangeade, Kümmel, cognac, cherry brandy, and
Russian anisette! 'A liquid *Jezebel*,' little Madame de Lizery
(Robert Parville's mistress) had exclaimed, and then told me

that at Les Oiseaux the girls, well up in *Athalie*, used to call all '*horribles mélanges*' Jezebels.

'Well, Claudine, aren't you going to say anything to me about my at-home day?'

'Your at-home day, my poor sweet! I think you're as much to be pitied as censured . . . and that we must open the windows. Several of these little walnut cream cakes left over look quite appetizing. Are you sure nobody's "wiped their feet on them", as my noble father would say?'

Renaud shook his head and pressed his temples. He could feel migraine threatening.

'Your noble father always shows commendable prudence. Follow his example and don't touch those dubious cakes. I saw Suzanne de Lizery brush her hands over them, hands that had just been touching goodness knows what and had been "in mourning" a good while, judging by their black-rimmed nails.'

'Ugh! . . . Shut up or I shan't be able to eat my dinner. Let's go into the dressing-room.'

My husband had received so many people that I felt abominably tired. But he – young Renaud with the silver hair – seemed more animated than ever. He wandered about, chattering and laughing, inhaled deep breaths of my person (which apparently drove away any hint of migraine), and kept circling round my chair.

'Why *do* you keep on gyrating like a buzzard?'

'A buzzard, eh? I've no idea what a buzzard is. Let me guess . . . I imagine the buzzard as a little animal with a hooked nose . . . Buzzard! A little chestnut beast that kicks with its hooves and has a horrid disposition. Right?'

This picture of a four-legged bird-of-prey threw me into a paroxysm of such youthful gaiety that my husband stopped and stood still in front of me, almost offended. But I only laughed louder than ever and his eyes changed and became excited.

'My little curly shepherd, is it as funny as all that? Laugh again, so that I can see right to the back of your mouth.'

It was a warning! I was in danger of being made love to somewhat violently . . .

'No, really . . . not before dinner.'

'After?'

'I don't know.'

'Very well, before *and* after. Don't you admire my genius for compromise?'

Feeble, cowardly Claudine! There are certain kisses that are 'Sesames' . . . and after which I want to be conscious of nothing but darkness, nakedness, and the vain, silent struggle to hold myself back one minute, just one minute longer, on the edge of delight.

'Renaud, who *are* those people?'

Now that the light was out, I had sought my place in the bed, my place on his shoulder, where the rounded joint of the arm made me a soft, familiar bolster. Renaud stretched out his long legs and I cuddled my chilly feet against them; then he settled the back of his neck on the exact centre of the small pancake cushion, stuffed with horsehair, that serves him as a pillow. Invariably ritual preparations for the night, followed or preceded almost as regularly by other rites . . .

'What people, my own child?'

'The Rézis . . . the Lambrooks, I mean . . .'

'Ah! . . . I was sure you'd like the wife . . .'

'Tell me quick, who are they?'

'Well, they're a couple . . . charming, but ill-assorted. What I appreciate in the wife is a bosom and shoulders with milky blue veins that she displays at dinner parties. No young creature anxious to give pleasure to others could display more of them. Also an insinuating coquetry – of gesture, rather than word – and something gipsyish about her . . . a taste for pulling up her stakes and moving on. In the husband, what interested me was that inner collapse, disguised by his square shoulders and rigidly correct deportment. Colonel Lambrook has remained behind in the Colonies; all that has come back is his physical wreck. He goes on living a mysterious unknown life out there; the moment you mention his beloved India he stops answering you and immures himself in haughty silence. What magnet keeps him eternally fixed out there? Suffering, beauty, cruelty? No one knows. And it's such a rare thing, little girl, a mind so firmly sealed that it can keep its secret.'

61

Is it such a rare thing, dear Renaud?

'The first time I dined with them, a couple of years ago, in the fantastic bazaar that served them as a home at the time, they gave me an extremely attractive Burgundy. I asked whether I could get hold of some of it. "Yes," said Lambrook; "it isn't dear." He searched his memory for a moment, then raised his terra-cotta face and added: "Twenty rupees, I think." And he had been back in Europe ten years!'

I mused for a minute in silence, nestled against the warmth of my friend.

'Renaud, does he love his wife?'

'Maybe yes, maybe no. He treats her with a mixture of brutality and politeness that strikes me as sinister.'

'Is she unfaithful to him?'

'My darling bird, how on earth should I know?'

'Why, she might have been your mistress.'

The tone of conviction in which I said this convulsed Renaud with untimely mirth.

'Do keep still, or you'll have me on the floor. I've said nothing outrageous. There's nothing in the suggestion to shock either of you. Does she have women friends, do you know?'

'But this is an inquest . . . Why, it's worse, it's a conquest! Claudine, I've never seen you so interested in a woman you've met only once.'

'I admit it. Anyway, I'm getting myself into training. You accuse me of being unsociable, so I propose to make some acquaintances. And, as I've just met a pretty woman with an attractive voice and a hand that's pleasant to touch, I ask about her, I . . .'

'Claudine,' broke in Renaud, half teasing, half serious. 'Doesn't Rézi remind you a little of Luce? A resemblance that's more than . . . skin deep?'

The hateful man! Why deflower everything with a word? I turned over in one bound like a fish, and went off to seek sleep in the chaste and chilly regions of the far side of the great bed.

A big gap in my diary. I have not put down a daily account of my impressions and I am sure I should get them wrong in a general summing-up. Life goes on. It is cold. Renaud bustles about, in the highest spirits. He rushes me round from one first night to another, loudly proclaiming that the theatre bores him to tears, that the compulsory coarseness of the average play revolts him . . .

'Then why on earth do you go, Renaud?' asks the simple Claudine, genuinely puzzled.

'Simply . . . you'll despise me, my little judge . . . to see people. To see whether Annhine de Lys is still going with Miss Flossie; whether pretty Madame Mundoë's hat is a success, whether the strange, seductive Polaire with those eyes like an amorous gazelle's still holds the record in wasp-waists. To be there on the spot half an hour after midnight when Mendès is holding forth lyrically at a supper-table, *talking* his dazzling review. To blossom out myself in the presence of the grotesque old Barmann and her "cameleer", as Maugis calls Gréveuille. To admire the Field-Marshal's plume surmounting the face of that ferret run to fat, Madame de Saint-Niketês.'

No, I don't despise him for all that frivolity. And, besides, it wouldn't matter if I did, because I love him. I know that audiences at first nights never listen to the play. I do listen, I listen passionately . . . or else I say: 'This revolts me.' Renaud envies me such simple and emphatic convictions: 'You're young, my little girl . . .' Not as young as he is! He makes love to me, works, visits people, gossips, dines out, gives a party at home at four every Friday, and finds time to choose a sealskin jacket for me. From time to time, when we are by ourselves, he relaxes his charming, tired face, holds me close against him and sighs, with profound unhappiness: 'Claudine, my darling child, how old I am! I can feel the minutes adding wrinkles one by one, and that hurts, that hurts so much!' If only he knew how I adored him like that, and how I hope that the years will calm his fever for showing-off! Only then, when he'll be willing to stop parading and throwing out his chest, shall we at last come together completely. Only then shall I stop panting with the effort to keep up with his forty-five-year-old's gallop.

SIX

ONE DAY, WITH an amused memory of the Andalusian
sculptor and his 'You are a swine, Madame!' I decided to
discover the Louvre and to admire these new Rubenses
without a guide. Wearing my sealskin bolero jacket and the
matching toque that looks as if a little animal were curled up
asleep on my head, I set off boldly on my own. Having not a
scrap of sense of direction I kept getting lost at every turning
of the gallery like a wedding-party in a Zola novel. For
though, in a wood, I know by instinct where the east lies and
what time it is, I go astray in a suite of rooms all on one floor.

I found the Rubenses. They disgusted me. Just that, they
disgusted me! I tried loyally, for a good half-hour, to work
myself up into a state of excitement about them, but no! That
meat, all that meat; that heavy-jowled powdered Marie de'
Medici with her sweating breasts, that plump warrior, her
husband, being carried away by a victorious and robust –
Zephyr . . . no, no, *no*! I shall never understand. If Renaud
and Renaud's female friends knew that! . . . Well, it can't be
helped! If I'm pushed, I shall say what I think.

Depressed, I walked away, taking small steps to avoid the
temptation of sliding on the polished parquet between the
rows of masterpieces observing me.

Ah! here was something better, some Spanish and Italian
fellows really worth looking at. All the same, it was cheek of
them to put the label 'St John the Baptist' on that seductive
painted face by Da Vinci, drooped forward and smiling like
Mademoiselle Moreno.

Heavens, what a beautiful young man! I had discovered, quite by chance, the boy who could have made me commit sin. Luckily he was only on canvas! Who was he? 'Portrait of a Sculptor', by Bronzino. I wanted to touch that forehead, just where it swelled above the eyebrows under the thick black hair, and that ruthless, undulating lip; I wanted to kiss those eyes that looked like a cynical page's. Did that white, naked hand really model statuettes? I imagined that the downless skin was of the kind that darkens to the colour of old ivory under the armpits and in the hollows behind the knees . . . A skin that would be warm all over, even on the calves . . . And the palms of the hands would be moist . . .

Whatever was I doing? Blushing, and only half-awake, I looked about me . . . What was I doing? I was being unfaithful to Renaud!

I shall have to tell Rézi about this aesthetic adultery. She will laugh, with that laugh that breaks out suddenly and dies away listlessly. For we are two good friends, Rézi and I. A fortnight has been enough to make us so; it is what Renaud would call 'an agelong intimacy'.

Two good friends, yes indeed. I am enchanted by her. She is fascinated by me. Nevertheless, we do not really confide in each other. No doubt, it is still a little too soon for that. Too soon for me, very definitely. Rézi does not deserve Claudine's inmost soul. I give her my physical presence, my short, curly hair that it amuses her to 'do' – vain effort! – and my face that she seems to love without any hint of jealousy when she takes it between her two soft hands to 'watch my eyes dance', as she says.

She treats me freely to her beauty and grace, with an insistent coquetry. For the past few days, I have been going to see her every morning at eleven.

The Lambrooks live in the avenue Kléber, in one of those modern flats where so much space has been sacrificed to the concierge and the staircase, the front and back drawing-rooms – rather fine panelling, a good copy of Van Loo's portrait of Louis XV as a child – that the private rooms have to snatch air and daylight as best they can. Rézi sleeps in a long, dark bedroom and dresses in a gallery. But I like this inconvenient, perpetually overheated dressing-room. And Rézi dresses and undresses in it by a kind of magical process. Sitting very demurely in a low armchair, I watch her admiringly.

While still in her chemise, she does her hair. That marvellous hair, tinted pink by the blinding electric light, green by the low streak of blue daylight, shimmers when she tosses her head to shake it out. At all hours of the day, this false double light from the inadequate window and the over-bright bulbs illuminates Rézi with a theatrical glare.

She brushes her dancing cloud of hair . . . A wave of her wand and, in a flash, thanks to a magic comb, all that gold is gathered up into a shining twisted knot on the nape of her neck, with every ripple subdued. How on earth does it stay put? Wide-eyed, I am on the verge of imploring: 'Do it again!' Rézi does not wait for my request. Another wave of the wand and the pretty woman in the chemise rises up, sheathed in a dark cloth dress and wearing a hat, ready to go out. The straitlaced corsets, the impertinent knickers, the soft and silent petticoat, have flung themselves on her like eager birds. Then Rézi gives me a triumphant look and laughs.

Her undressing is just as magical. The garments drop all at once, as if they were stuck together, and this charming creature retains nothing but her chemise . . . and her hat. How that irritates me and amazes me! She pins it on her head before she puts on her corsets, she leaves it on till she has taken off her stockings. She wears a hat in her bath, she tells me.

'But why this worship of headgear?'

'I don't know. Something to do with modesty, perhaps. If I had to escape in the middle of the night because the house was on fire, I wouldn't mind running out in the street completely naked, but not without a hat.'

'Honestly? The firemen would have a treat!'

She is prettier and not so tall as my first impression suggested; small, but perfectly proportioned, with a white skin that rarely flushes to pink. Her short-sightedness, the changeable grey of her eyes and her fluttering eyelashes dissemble her thoughts. In fact, I do not know her at all, in spite of the spontaneous sudden way she came out at our fourth meeting, with this:

'I'm crazy about three things, Claudine: travelling, Paris . . . and you.'

She was born in Paris and loves it like a foreigner; she has a passion for its cold, dubious smell, for the hour when the gaslight reddens the blue dusk, for its theatres and its streets.

'Nowhere else in the world, Claudine, are the women as pretty as they are in Paris! (Let's leave Montigny out of it, darling . . .) It's in Paris that you see the most fascinating faces whose beauty is waning – women of forty, frantically made-up and tight-laced, who have kept their delicate noses and eyes like a young girl's. Women who let themselves be stared at with a mixture of pleasure and bitterness.'

A woman who thinks and talks like that is not a fool. That day, I seized hold of her pointed fingers that were drawing invisible spirals to illustrate what she was saying, as if to thank her for having charming thoughts. The next day she was in a flutter of ecstasy over Liberty's window display, a facile colour harmony of pink and saffron satins!

I regularly stay later than I mean to at the avenue Kléber, and it is just noon when I reluctantly decide to leave the low armchair and return home to my husband and my lunch. I am in no hurry to get back to Renaud's eager embraces and his appetite for red meat (for he doesn't live as I do, on quails and bananas). Almost every day, just as I am about to go, the door of the dressing-room opens noiselessly and reveals the deceptively robust figure of Lambrook framed in the doorway. It happened again yesterday . . .

'Wherever did you spring from?' exclaimed Rézi irritably.

'From the avenue des Champs Élysées,' replied the phlegmatic man. Then he hung about, kissing my hand, inspecting my unfastened jacket, staring at Rézi in her corsets and finally said to his wife:

'My dear, what a lot of time you waste dolling yourself up!'

Thinking of my friend's fantastic speed in dressing, I burst out laughing. Lambrook did not blink, but his terracotta skin faintly darkened. He asked how Renaud was, hoped we should both come and dine with him soon, and went away.

'Rézi, whatever's the matter with him?'

'Nothing. But don't laugh at him, Claudine, when he's talking to me; he thinks you're making fun of him.'

'Really? I don't care if he does.'

'But I do. It means I shall have a scene with him . . . His jealousy gets me down.'

'Jealous of *me*! On what grounds? Is the man out of his senses?'

'He doesn't like me having a woman friend . . .'

Might he have his reasons, the husband?

Yet nothing in Rézi's behaviour leads me to think so . . . Sometimes she looks at me for a long while without blinking her short-sighted eyes, whose eyelids are almost parallel – a detail that makes them seem longer – and her thin, tight-shut mouth half opens and becomes childish and tempting. A little shiver runs over her shoulders, she gives a nervous laugh and exclaims: 'Someone's walking over my grave!' . . . and kisses me. That is all. It would show considerable vanity on my part if I imagined . . .

I encourage nothing. I let time slip by, I study every subtle shade and shimmer of this rainbow-like Rézi, and I wait for what will come. I wait, I wait . . . more out of laziness than virtue.

I saw Rézi this morning. That did not stop her from rushing around to me about five o'clock, all impatience. She sat down, just as Fanchette lies down, after turning right round twice. Her dark blue tailor-made gave her golden hair a reddish tinge; a complicated feather hat crowned her with embattled grey seagulls, so swirling with life that I should not have been greatly surprised to hear those entangled beaks twittering.

She installed herself, like someone taking refuge, and sighed.

'What's the matter, Rézi?'

'Nothing. I'm bored at home. The people who come to see me there bore me. One admirer, two admirers, three admirers today . . . I've seen enough of them! The monotony of those men. I nearly hit the third one!'

'Why the third?'

'Because he told me, half an hour after the second – and in exactly the same terms, the tiresome creature – that he loved me! And the second had already been a repetition of the first. That trio will be seeing precious little of me in future. Oh Lord, all those men, all exactly alike!'

'Only take one of them; you'd get more variety.'

'I'd get more exhausted too.'

'But . . . your husband . . . doesn't he make a fuss?'

'He doesn't turn a hair. What makes you think he would?'

Honestly, did she take me for an utter fool? What about all those precautions the other morning, those warnings full of dark hints? Yet she was looking at me with her clearest, most candid gaze, her eyes shot with gleams of moonstones and grey pearls.

'Now, come, Rézi! The day before yesterday, I mustn't even laugh at what he said . . .'

'Ah!' (Her hand twirled gracefully in the air, as if she were whipping up an invisible mayonnaise.) 'But, Claudine, that's not at all the same thing . . . these men who buzz round me . . . and you.'

'I should hope not! And since your reasons for liking me can't be the same as theirs . . .'

She gave me a sudden swift glance, then promptly looked away.

'. . . you might at least tell me, Rézi, why you don't dislike seeing me.'

Reassured, she put down her muff, so as to be freer to use her hands, her neck and her whole torso to emphasize what she wanted to tell me; she settled herself deeper in the big armchair and gave me an affectionate, mysterious smile.

'Why do I like you, Claudine? I could simply tell you: "Because I think you're pretty," and that would be enough for me, but it wouldn't be enough for your pride . . . Why am I fond of you? Because your eyes and your hair are made of the same metal, and they're all that remain of a little light bronze statue; the rest has turned into flesh. Because your harsh gestures make a good accompaniment to your soft voice; because you tone down your fierceness for me; because, whenever one guesses one of your secret thoughts or you let one out, you blush as if someone had slipped a rude hand under your skirt . . .'

I interrupted her with a gesture – yes, it was a harsh one. I was irritated and disturbed that so much of myself should show through without my knowledge . . . Was I going to be angry? To leave her altogether? She forestalled any hostile resolve by kissing me impetuously, close to my ear. Drowned in fur, brushed by pointed wings, I hardly had time to be conscious of Rézi's own smell and the deceptive simplicity of her scent – when Renaud came in.

I leant back, embarrassed, in the chair. Embarrassed, not by Rézi's swift kiss, but by Renaud's keen look and the amused, almost encouraging indulgence I read in it. He kissed my friend's hand, saying:

'Please don't let me disturb anything.'

'But you're not disturbing anything at all,' she cried. 'Anything or anyone! On the contrary, you can help me make Claudine stop frowning. She's angry because I've just paid her a very sincere compliment.'

'Very sincere, I'm sure, but did you put enough conviction into your tone? My Claudine is a very serious and very passionate little girl, who's incapable of accepting . . .' (here, because he belonged to a generation that still read Musset, he hummed the accompaniment to the serenade from *Don Juan*) . . . 'who's incapable of accepting certain words if they're underlined by certain smiles.'

'Renaud, I implore you, no marital revelations!'

In spite of myself, I had raised my voice in exasperation, but Rézi turned her most disarming smile on me.

'Oh, *yes*, oh *yes*, Claudine! Do let him tell. I take a very real interest in them and it's an act of charity to let my ears have a little dissipation! They're getting to the point of forgetting what the word "love" means.'

Hmm! This excited eagerness of a sex-starved wife struck me as coming rather oddly after her recent assurance that she was sick and tired of men wanting to make love to her. However, Renaud knew nothing of that. Moved with generous compassion, he studied Rézi from her chignon to her ankles and it was impossible for me not to laugh when he exclaimed:

70

'Poor child! So young, and already deprived of what gives beauty and colour to life! Come to me. Consolation awaits you on the couch in my study, I am prepared to sacrifice myself – and it'll cost you less than going to a specialist!'

'Cost me less? I'm suspicious of reduced fees to the profession.'

'You're not a professional. Besides, either one's a man of honour or one isn't . . .'

'And you aren't? Thanks, no!'

'You shall give me . . . whatever you like.'

'Whatever I like?' She half-veiled her smoke-coloured eyes. 'Well . . . perhaps you might amuse yourself with a little preliminary trifling.'

'I should be only too delighted to trifle with you.'

Enchanted at feeling a little outraged, Rézi arched her neck and tucked in her chin, exactly as Fanchette does when she finds an exceptionally large grasshopper or a stag-beetle in her path.

'No, I tell you, benefactor of humanity! In any case, I haven't got to that stage yet!'

'And what stage have you got to . . . already?'

'To compensations.'

'Which particular ones? There are so many species – at least two.'

She turned pink, overdid her short-sightedness, then, with a little twist, turned to me, imploring:

'Claudine, protect me!'

'I'll protect you all right . . . by forbidding you to let Renaud console you.'

'Why, I believe you're really jealous! Are you?'

She sparkled with a malicious delight that immensely enhanced her beauty. Poised on the edge of her chair, with one leg outstretched and the other bent back and clearly outlined under her skirt, she leant towards me in a tense attitude, as if about to run. Her cheek, close to mine, was gilded with a down paler than her hair, and her eyelashes fluttered incessantly, transparent as a wasp's gauzy wings. Overcome with so much beauty, it was with the utmost sincerity that I replied:

'Jealous? Oh, no, Rézi; you're far too pretty! I'd never forgive Renaud for being unfaithful to me with an ugly woman.'

Renaud caressed me with one of those intelligent looks that bring me back to him when my fierce unsociability or an unusual sharp attack of loneliness and abstraction have carried me rather far away . . . I was grateful to him for saying so many loving things to me like that, in silence, over Rézi's head . . .

However, Rézi-the-Golden (had she entirely understood me?) drew herself upright, gave a nervous stretch with her hands clasped inside her muff, made a face and said, with a little snort:

'Oh dear . . . your complicated psychology has made me feel quite faint, and I'm awfully hungry.'

'Oh, my poor dear! And here have I been letting you starve!'

I leapt up and rushed to the bell.

A little while later, peace and friendly understanding exhaled from steaming cups and slices of toast slowly soaking up butter. But personally I despised those smart people's tea. With a basket in my lap, I was peeling withered apples and pricking and squeezing flabby medlars, winter fruits from home sent me by Mélie that smell of store-cupboards and over-ripeness.

And because a piece of burnt and blackened toast was making the room smell of creosote and fresh coal, off I went on the wings of imagination to Montigny, to the big open fireplace with the canopy over it . . . I thought I could see Mélie throwing a damp faggot on it, and Fanchette sitting on the raised hearthstone, shift back a little, shocked by the boldness of the flames and the crackling of the green wood . . .

'My own girl!'

I had been dreaming aloud. And, at the sight of Renaud's mirth and Rézi's stupefaction, I flushed and gave a shame-faced laugh.

SEVEN

THE MILD WINTER drags on, warm and enervating. January is nearly over. The days go by, alternating between a feverish rush and incredible idleness. Theatres, dinners, matinées, and concerts, up to one o'clock in the morning, often two! Renaud struts, throws out his chest, and I sag and wilt.

I wake up late, in a bed submerged under newspapers. Renaud divides his attention between 'the attitude of England' and that of Claudine, lying on her stomach and lost in hostile dreams, trying to catch up on the indispensable sleep of which artificial life deprives her. Luncheon is a brief affair of red meat for Renaud and various sugary horrors for myself. From two to five, the programme varies.

What does not vary is the five o'clock visit to Rézi or from Rézi; she is becoming more and more attached to me without trying to hide it. And I am becoming attached to her, God knows, but I conceal it . . .

Almost every evening, at seven o'clock, coming away from a tea-shop or a bar where Rézi revives herself with a cocktail and I nibble potato chips with too much salt on them, I think with silent fury that I have got to go home and dress and that Renaud is already waiting for me, adjusting his pearl studs. Thanks to my convenient short hair, I have to admit – my modesty blushes! – that men and women find me equally disturbing.

Because of my shorn mane and my coldness towards them, men say to themselves: 'She only goes in for women.' For it is obvious to the meanest understanding that, if I don't like men,

73

I *must* be pursuing women; such is the simplicity of the masculine mind!

Moreover, the women – on account of my shorn mane and my coldness towards their husbands and lovers – seem inclined to think as they do. I have caught charming glances in my direction; curious, shamed, fugitive glances and even blushes if I let my eyes rest for a moment on the grace of a bare shoulder or a perfect neck. I have also sustained the shock of extremely explicit approaches; but these drawing-room professionals – the square lady of fifty or more; the thin, dark little girl with the flat behind; the monocled Jewess who plunges her sharp nose into *décolletages* as if she expected to find a lost ring in them – these temptresses found Claudine so lacking in response that they were obviously shocked. And that nearly ruined my promising reputation. To make up for it, the night before last, I saw one of my 'women friends' (i.e. a young literary lady I had met five times) give such a malicious smile when she mentioned Rézi's name that I understood the implication only too well. And I thought that Rézi's husband might 'cut up rough' the day rumours began to reach his brick-red ear.

A letter from Papa arrived for me, grandiloquent and heart-broken. In spite of the active bee that buzzes incessantly in his bonnet and keeps him happy, Papa is getting upset by my absence. In Paris, it didn't worry him in the least. But down there he has found the old house empty, empty of Claudine. No more silent little girl curled up, with a book on her knees, in the hollow of a big armchair bursting at the seams – or perched in the fork of the walnut-tree, shelling nuts with a noise like a squirrel – or stretched full length on the top of a wall with a predatory eye on the next-door neighbour's plums and old Madame Adolphe's dahlias . . . Papa doesn't *say* all this; his dignity forbids it, as does the nobility of his style which does not condescend to such puerilities. But he thinks it. So do I.

Thoroughly upset, brimming over with memories and regrets, I rushed to Renaud to hide myself in the hollow of his shoulder and find oblivion there. My dear giant, whom I was distracting (without his grumbling) from virtuous industry, does not always understand the causes of what he calls 'my shipwrecks'. But as usual, he sheltered me generously, without asking too many questions. In his warmth, the mirage of Fresnois melted into a mist and vanished. And when, swiftly excited by holding me close, he tightened his embrace and bent down his gold-streaked moustache that smelt of Egyptian tobacco, I was able to look up at him and laugh.

'You smell like a blonde who smokes!' I told him.

This time he retorted, teasingly:

'And Rézi, what does she smell of?'

'Rézi?' . . . (I thought for a moment.) 'She smells of untruthfulness.'

'Untruthfulness! Are you trying to make out that she doesn't love you and is pretending to have a crush on you?'

'No, I'm not. I said more than I meant to. Rézi doesn't lie; she dissimulates. She shuts things away at the back of her mind. She isn't like the pretty Van Langendonck, who informs you, with a wealth of detail, "I've just come from the Galeries Lafayette" at the beginning of a sentence that ends up: "Five minutes ago I was at Saint-Pierre de Montrouge." Rézi doesn't gush, and I'm thankful that she doesn't. But I *feel* that she hides things, that she decently buries any number of little horrors, pawing away as scrupulously as Fanchette in her tray. Commonplace little horrors, if you like, but symmetrically neat.'

'What makes you so sure?'

'Nothing, of course, if you need proofs! I'm going by my instincts. There's another thing – her maid often has a way of coming in the morning, giving her a crumpled piece of paper and saying: "Madame left this in yesterday's pocket . . ." By chance, I happened one day to glance at the crushed-up contents of "yesterday's pocket" and I can assure you that the envelope was still unopened. What do you think of that as a postal system? The suspicious Lambrook himself would think it was nothing but an old bit of paper.'

'It's ingenious,' mused Renaud aloud.

'So you realize, my dear giant, that this secretive Rézi who turns up here all white and gold, with eyes so clear you can see right to the bottom of them, who envelops me with a pastoral scent of fern and iris . . .'

'Oho! Claudine!'

'Whatever's come over you?'

'Come over *me*, indeed? What about *you*? Am I dreaming? What, my remote, disdainful Claudine getting interested in someone, in Rézi, to the point of studying her, to the point of thinking deeply about her and making deductions! Now then, Mademoiselle' (he was scolding me in jest, with his arms folded, like Papa). 'Now then, isn't it a fact that we are in love?'

I drew sharply away from him and glared at him from under such frowning eyebrows that he was startled.

'What? Angry again? Really, you do take everything tragically!'

'And you don't take anything seriously!'

'Only one thing: you . . .'

He waited expectantly, but I did not budge.

'Come here, my little silly! Come here, then! What a lot of trouble I have with this child! Claudine,' he asked (I was sitting on his knee again, silent and still a little tense), 'tell me one thing.'

'What?'

'Why, when it comes to admitting one of your secret thoughts, even to your old husband-papa, do you jib so fiercely? You couldn't show more outraged modesty if you were asked to display your behind at an imposing gathering of Paris celebrities. In fact, I believe you'd show less.'

'Dear, simple man, that's because I *know* my behind, which is firm, pleasantly coloured and agreeable to touch. I am not so confident about my thoughts, about their clarity and the welcome they'll receive . . . My modesty is very clear-sighted; its job is to hide anything in me that I'm afraid might be ugly and weak.'

I surprised Renaud this morning in a fierce and gloomy rage. In silence I watched him throwing balls of screwed-up paper on the fire, then suddenly sweep a whole pile of pamphlets off his desk and toss the lot on the spluttering coke. A little ashtray, hurled with a deadly aim, buried itself in the waste-paper basket. Next to it was the priestlike Ernest who came in for his wrath and, because he had not appeared the moment the bell rang, heard himself threatened with instant dismissal like a mere layman. Things were hotting up!

I sat down, with my hands folded, looking on and waiting. Renaud's eyes discovered me and softened:

'Why, you're back, my sweet. I didn't see you. Where have you been?'

'At Rézi's.'

'I ought to have known that! . . . But forgive me for being absent-minded, darling. I'm annoyed.'

'Lucky you hide it so well!'

'Don't laugh . . . Come over here, close to me. Soothe me. I've had some infuriating, quite odious news about Marcel . . .'

'Oh?'

I thought of my stepson's last visit. He really is going too far. An incredible desire to swagger drove him to tell me a hundred things I had not asked him, among others a fairly detailed account of an encounter in the rue de la Pompe, at the time when the Lycée Janson releases a convey of boys in blue berets into the street . . . That particular day, Marcel's Odyssey was interrupted by Rézi, who, for a good three-quarters of an hour, wasted all her wiles on him, vainly trying the whole armoury of her glances and a series of her most alluring swirls. Finding all her weapons blunt, she finally wearied of the fight and gave it up. She turned to me with a pretty gesture of discouragement that so plainly said: 'Ouf! I've had enough!' that I began to laugh and Marcel (that pervert is far from being a fool) smiled with infinite disdain.

This disdain quickly changed to undisguised curiosity when he saw the eclectic Rézi bring all the same battery of allurements to bear on me . . . At that, with an ill-timed pretence of being tactful, he left.

What new prank had that boy been up to?

With my head resting on Renaud's knees, I waited to be enlightened.

'Always the same story, my poor darling. My charming son is bombarding some brat of good family with neo-Greek

77

literature . . . You don't say anything, my little girl? I ought to be used to it by now, alas! But these affairs make my gorge rise. I find them utterly revolting.'

'Why?'

Renaud started at my quietly asked question.

'What do you mean? Why?'

'What I meant, my dear man, was why do you smile excitedly, almost approvingly, at the idea that Luce was too loving a friend to me? . . . And at the hope . . . I repeat, the hope! . . . that Rézi might become a luckier Luce?'

How very odd my husband's face looked at that moment! Extreme surprise, a kind of shocked prudery, a shamefaced, ingratiating smile passed over it in waves like cloud-shadows running over a meadow . . . Finally, he exclaimed triumphantly:

'That's not the same thing!'

'Thank heavens, no, not quite . . .'

'No, it isn't at all the same thing! You women can do anything. It's charming and it's of no consequence whatever . . .'

'No consequence? . . . I don't agree with you.'

'I mean what I say and I'm right! Between you pretty little animals it's a . . . how can I put it? . . . a consolation for *us*, a restful change . . .'

'Oh?'

'. . . or, at least, a kind of compensation. It's the logical search for a more perfect partner, for a beauty more like your own, which reflects your own sensitiveness and your own weaknesses . . . If I dared (but I shouldn't dare), I would say that certain women need women in order to preserve their taste for men.'

Frankly, no, I did *not* understand! How singularly painful it is to love each other as much as we do and to feel so differently! . . . I could only see what my husband had just said as a paradox that flattered and disguised the touch of the *voyeur* in his sexual make-up.

Rézi has turned herself into my shadow. She is there at all hours of the day, lassoing me with her harmonious gestures whose line prolongs itself into the void, throwing a spell over me with her words, her looks, her stormy thoughts that I expect to see bursting out in sparks from the tips of her tapering fingers . . . I am getting uneasy, I am conscious of a will in her more consistent, more obstinate than my own which goes by leaps and bounds and then turns sluggish.

Sometimes, irritated and enervated by her soft persistence, by her beauty that she flourishes under my nose like a bouquet and adorns, barely veiled, before my eyes, I feel like asking her abruptly: 'What are you driving at?' But I am frightened that she might tell me. And I prefer to keep a cowardly silence, so as to be able to stay with her with a clear conscience, for, during the last three months, she has become my cherished habit.

Indeed, apart from the insistence of her soft grey eyes and the 'Heavens! how I love you!' she often lets out as innocently and spontaneously as a little girl, there is nothing I need to be scared about.

In actual fact, what is it she loves in me? I am perfectly aware of the genuineness, if not of her affection, at least of her desire. And I am afraid, yes, afraid already – that this desire is the only thing that animates her.

Yesterday, blinded by a migraine and oppressed by the twilight, I let Rézi lay her hands over my eyes. With my lids closed, I could imagine the supple curve of her body leaning over me, slim in a clinging dress of a leaden grey that made one uncertain of the exact colour of her eyes.

A dangerous silence descended on us both. Nevertheless, she did not risk a gesture and she did not kiss me. After some minutes, she just said: 'Oh my dear, my dear . . .' and fell silent again.

When the clock struck seven, I shook myself sharply and rushed to the switch to turn on the light. Rézi's smile, revealed pale and enchanting in the sudden glare, encountered my harshest, most forbidding face. Repressing a little sigh, she picked up her gloves with a supple movement, straightened her irremovable hat, murmured 'Good-bye' and 'Till tomorrow' into my neck, and I found myself alone in front of a mirror, listening to her light escaping footsteps.

Don't lie to yourself, Claudine! That meditation of yours, leaning on your elbows in front of that glass, with that air of suppressing remorse, was it anything else but the pleasure of verifying that your face was still intact – that face with the Havana-brown eyes, that face Rézi loves?

EIGHT

'MY DARLING LITTLE girl, what are you thinking about?'
His darling little girl was squatting, tailor-fashion, on the big
bed she had not yet quitted . . . Enveloped in a vast pink
nightdress, she was thoughtfully cutting the toe-nails of her
right foot with a pretty pair of ivory-handled clippers and not
breathing a word.

'My darling little girl, what are you thinking about?'

I raised my head, adorned with snaky curls, and I stared at
Renaud – who, already dressed, was knotting his tie – as if I
had never set eyes on him before.

'Yes, what are you thinking about? Ever since we woke up,
you haven't said a word to me. You let me prove my affection
without even noticing it.'

I raised a protesting hand.

'Obviously, I'm exaggerating. But you were decidedly
absent-minded, Claudine . . .'

'You amaze me!'

'Not as much as you amaze me! I'm used to your showing
more consciousness during these diversions.'

'They're not diversions.'

'Call them nightmares, if you like, but my remark holds
good. Where have you been wandering all the morning, my
bird?'

'I'd like to go to the country,' I said, upon reflection.

'Oh!' he exclaimed in consternation. 'Claudine! Just look!'

He raised the curtain; a deluge was streaming down on the
roofs and overflowing gutters.

'This morning dew whetted your appetite for it? Conjure up dirty water running all over the ground, the bottom of your skirt clinging to your ankles; think of cold drops dripping off the lobes of your ears . . .'

'I am thinking of it. You've never understood the first thing about country rain, about *sabots* that go "sluck" when they leave their wet imprints. Or about the rough hood with a bead of water stuck on the end of every woolly hair, the pointed hood that makes a little house for your face that you snuggle into and laugh . . . Of course, the cold stings, but you warm your thighs with two pocketfuls of hot chestnuts and you wear thick, knitted gloves.'

'Don't go on! My teeth are on edge at the thought of woollen gloves rasping against the ends of my finger-nails! If you want to see your Montigny again, if you've really set your heart on it as much as all that, if it's a "last wish"' . . . (he sighed) . . . 'we'll go.'

No, we won't go. Talking out loud, I had sincerely found myself thinking the words I was saying. But that morning, I was not tormented by regret for Fresnois; my silence was not due to homesickness. There was something else on my mind.

It was that . . . that hostilities had commenced and that, confronted with Rézi's amorous treachery, I found myself irresolute, without any plan of defence.

I had gone to see her at five o'clock, because, at the moment, half my life is spent in her company. And this enrages me and fascinates me and I can do nothing about it.

I found her all alone, roasting herself at a fire like the fires of hell. The glare from the hearth seemed to glow right through her, turning her tousled hair into a halo of pink flames, blurring the lines of her figure to a haze of coppery red and the crimson of molten metal. She smiled at me without getting up and held out her arms to me so lovingly that I took fright and only kissed her once.

'All alone, Rézi?'

'No. I was with you.'

'With me . . . and who else?'

'With you . . . and me. I don't want anything more. But it isn't enough for you, I realize that.'

'You're wrong, darling.'

She shook her head with a swaying movement that rippled right down to her feet, tucked in under a low pouffe. And the gentle, dreamy face, where the bright flame carved two dimples of shadow at the corners of the mouth, looked long and searchingly into mine.

So, it had come to a head! And was that all I could find to say? Couldn't I, before letting her overwhelm me and permeate herself with me, have had it out with her, clearly and explicitly? Rézi was not a Luce whom you could beat, who would leave you in peace for twenty-four hours if you smacked her. It was my fault; it was all my fault . . .

She gazed up at me sadly and thoughtfully and said, hardly above a whisper:

'Oh, Claudine, why are you so suspicious of me? When I sit close to you, I always find a defensive leg, stiff as a chair-leg, thrust out under your skirt to stop me coming nearer. It's unkind of me, Claudine, to think you have to put up a physical defence! Have I ever let my mouth make one of these deliberate mistakes, pretending afterwards I was in such a hurry or it was so dark I couldn't be sure where your face was? You've treated me like a . . . a diseased person, like a . . . a professional, whose hands you keep watching, who makes you self-conscious about your every movement . . .'

She stopped and waited. I said nothing. She went on, with a more tender approach:

'My dear, my dear. Is this really you, the intelligent, sensitive Claudine who's setting these conventional limits to love? They're so ridiculous!'

'Ridiculous?'

'Yes, there's no other word. You're my friend; you've only to kiss me here and here. You're my lover; you can kiss me wherever you like.'

'Rézi . . .'

She checked my incipient gesture.

'Oh, don't be frightened! There's nothing of *that* sort between us. But I wish, dear, that you'd stop hurting me and setting your modesty up in arms against me, because I don't deserve it. Be fair to me,' she implored (she had crept closer to me without my noticing it, with an invisible, snakelike slither). 'What is it about my fondness for you that puts you on the defensive?'

'Your thoughts,' I said in a low voice.

She was close to me, close enough for me to feel the warmth she had received from the fire radiating on my cheek.

'Then I ask your forgiveness,' she whispered, 'for an affection too strong for me to disguise . . .'

She seemed docile, almost resigned. My breath, that I drew more slowly so that she should not guess I was in the least disturbed, brought me her smell of overheated silk and iris, a smell even sweeter because she had raised her arm to smooth the golden coil on her nape . . . What could stop me from losing my head? . . . Pride restrained me from trumping up some obvious excuse to make a diversion. Rézi sighed and stretched her arms . . . Her husband had just come in, in that silent, indiscreet way of his.

'What, no light yet, Rézi, my dear?' he said with apparent astonishment, after he had shaken her hands.

'Oh, don't ring!' I begged, without waiting for Rézi to answer. 'It's the time I love, the hour between the dog and the wolf, as we say in France.'

'It strikes me as considerably nearer the wolf than the dog,' that insupportable man replied very quietly.

Rézi, obstinately silent, followed him with a look of black hatred. He walked away with an even tread, entered the zone of shadow in the open doorway of the great drawing-room and continued his promenade. His measured step brought him back to us, right in front of the fire that lit up his hard face and opaque eyes from below. Having come within six inches of me, he made a military half-turn and walked away again.

I remained seated, not knowing what to do.

Rézi's eyes became diabolical; she calculated her spring . . . Rearing up with a swift, silent movement, she pounced on me, mastering me with a fantastically soft mouth and an arm round my neck. Above my own, her wide-open eyes listened to the retreating footsteps and her free hand, held high, marked the rhythm of her husband's walk and of the quivering of her own lips that seemed to be counting my heart-beats: one, two, three, four, five . . . Like a snapped link, the embrace broke off; Lambrook turned round; Rézi was once again sitting at my feet, apparently seeing pictures in the fire.

In my indignation, my surprise, my anxiety about the real risk she had just run, I could not suppress a shuddering sigh and a cry of distress.

'You were saying, dear lady?'

'Why, dear sir, only that you must throw me out at once! It's appallingly late . . . Renaud must be looking for me in the Morgue!'

'I flatter myself that he would look for you here first.'

I could have hit that man!

'Rézi . . . good-bye . . .'

'See you tomorrow, darling?'

'Yes. Till then.'

And that is why Claudine was so pensive this morning, as she cut the toenails of her right foot.

Cowardly Rézi! The expertness of her gesture; the abuse she made of my discretion, knowing she could rely on it; the unforgettable perfection of the perilous kiss, all that yesterday plunged me into deep and heavy thoughts. And Renaud thought I was depressed. Doesn't he know then, will he never know, that in my eyes, desire, vivid and recent regret and sensual pleasure are all invariably tinged with sombre hues?

Lying Rézi! Liar! Two minutes before the assault of her kiss, her humble, sincere voice had been reassuring me, telling me how hurt she was by my unjust suspicion. Liar!

In my innermost self, the suddenness of her trap pleaded in her favour. This Rézi, who had complained that I might at least have appreciated her restraint, had not been afraid to reverse her decision all at once, to risk my anger and the jealousy of that hollow Colossus.

Which does she love better, danger or me?

Me, perhaps? Once again, I saw that animal spring of the loins, that thirsty gesture that flung her on my mouth . . . No, I would not go and see her today!

'Are you going out, Renaud? Will you take me with you?'

85

'With the greatest joy in the world, my charming child! Is Rézi engaged elsewhere, then?'

'Leave Rézi out of it. I want to go out with you.'

'A quarrel, already?'

I answered only with a gesture of fending something off and sweeping it away. He did not insist. Gracious as a loving woman, he hurried through his shopping in half an hour to rejoin me in the carriage – a hired coupé, a little shabby but well sprung – and drove me to Pépette's to drink tea and eat cheesecakes and lettuce and herring sandwiches . . . We were sitting there all warm and cosy, saying silly things to each other like a badly behaved young married couple . . . when my appetite and gaiety vanished simultaneously. Staring at a sandwich I had just bitten into, I had run up against a tiny, already distant memory.

One day, at Rézi's (it was barely two months ago) I had left a piece of toast, out of which I had bitten a half-moon-shaped slice . . . We were chatting and I did not notice Rézi's hand shyly and deftly steal that nibbled toast . . . But, all at once, I saw her fiercely biting it and enlarging the crescent marked by my teeth, and she realized that I had seen her. She blushed, and tried to save the situation by saying: 'Aren't I shockingly greedy!' That tiny incident, why did it rise up and trouble me at that moment? Suppose she were really unhappy because I hadn't come?

'Claudine! Hi, Claudine.'

'What?'

'But, my dear, this is a positive illness! There, there, my poor bird, the moment the fine weather comes, we'll go spanking off to Montigny, to your noble father, to Fanchette and Mélie! . . . I don't want to see you glooming like that, my precious child.'

I smiled at dear Renaud in an ambiguous way that did not reassure him in the least, and we returned home on foot in weather muggy after rain and with roads and pavements so greasy that horses and pedestrians staggered and slid with the same drunken unsteadiness.

At home, an express letter awaited me:

'Claudine, I implore you, forget, forget! Come back, so that

I can explain, if such a thing needs to be explained. It was a game, a bit of teasing, a wild desire to fool that person who kept on walking about so close to us and whose steps on the carpet exasperated me . . .'

What? Could I really believe my eyes? So, according to her, it was to fool 'that person who kept on walking about'? But I was the stupid idiot who had been fooled! 'A bit of teasing'? She would see if I could be teased in that sort of way with impunity!

My fury writhed inside me like a kitten sucking the teat; savage plans of revenge rushed through my mind . . . I refused to admit how much disappointment and jealousy there was in my rage . . . Renaud caught me unawares with the little blue letter open in my hands.

'Aha! She's given in? Splendid! Remember this, Claudine, it must always be the *other* who gives in!'

'You have such brilliant insight!'

My tone made him realize that I was in a stormy mood and he became anxious.

'Come now, what's happened? Anything you can tell me? I'm not asking for details.'

'Nothing to tell! You're right off the track. We've had a quarrel and that's all there is to it.'

'Would you like me to go round there and try to straighten things out?'

My poor, big man! His kindness and his unawareness relaxed me and I flung my arms round his neck with a laugh that had a touch of a sob in it.

'No, no. I'll go tomorrow. Calm yourself!'

'A bit of teasing!'

A remnant of common sense checked my hand as I was on the point of ringing Rézi's doorbell. But I know that common sense, because it is my own particular brand; it allows me, precisely one minute before fatal blunders, to enjoy the lucid pleasure of telling myself: 'This *is* a fatal blunder.' Fore-warned, I hurry on serenely towards disaster, steadied, like a ship well down in the water, by a reassuring load of total responsibility.

'Is Madame at home?'

'Madame is not very well, but she will be delighted to see Madame.'

Not very well? Hmmm! Not ill enough to stop me from saying what I intended to say! Anyway, all the better; it would make her feel worse. 'A game!' A game two people could play . . .

She was as white as her *crêpe-de-Chine* dress, her eyes ringed with a mauve border that made them look blue. Slightly startled and moved, furthermore, by her grace and the look she gave me, I stood still:

'Rézi, are you really ill?'

'No; not now I see you.'

I gave a rude shrug. Then I was utterly taken aback. For, seeing my sarcastic smile, she was suddenly beside herself with rage.

'You can laugh? Get out of here, if you want to laugh!'

Knocked off my high horse by this sudden violence, I tried to get into the saddle:

'You surprise me, my dear. I thought you had such a sense of humour, with your taste for *games*, for rather elaborate *bits of teasing*.'

'You did? You believed what I said? It isn't true. I lied when I wrote to you, out of pure cowardice, so as to see you again, because I can't do without you, but . . .'

Her eagerness melted into incipient tears.

'. . . but it wasn't a joke, Claudine!'

She waited, fearfully, for what I would say and was frightened by my silence. She did not know that everything in me was fluttering in wild confusion, like a nest of agitated birds, and that I was flooded with joy . . . Joy at being loved and hearing myself told so, a miser's joy at a treasure lost and recovered, victorious pride to feel I was something more than an exciting toy. It was the triumphant downfall of my feminine decency. I realized that . . . But because she loved me, I could make her suffer still more.

'Dear Rézi . . .'

'Ah! Claudine! . . .'

She believed I was on the verge of yielding completely; she

stood up, trembling all over, and held out her arms; her hair and her eyes glittered with the same pale fire . . . Alas! how the sight of anything I love, my friend's beauty, the soft shade of the Fresnois forests, Renaud's desire, always arouses in me the same craving to possess and embrace! Have I really only one mode of feeling? . . .

'Dear Rézi . . . am I to suppose, from the state you're in, that is the first time anyone has resisted you? When I look at you, I can so well understand that you must always have found women only too delighted and willing . . .'

Her arms, raised imploringly above the white dress that wound tightly about her, its train vanishing into the shadow like a mermaid's tail, dropped again. With her hands hanging limp, I saw her almost instantaneously recover her wits and turn angry again. She said defiantly:

'The first time? Do you imagine that after eight years of living with that hollow brick, my husband, I haven't tried everything? That, to kindle any spark of love in me, I haven't searched for the sweetest, most beautiful thing in the world, a loving woman? Perhaps what you value more than anything else is the novelty, the clumsiness of a first . . . transgression. Oh, Claudine, there is something better, there is deliberately seeking and choosing . . . I have chosen you,' she ended in a hurt voice, 'and you have only put up with me . . .'

A last grain of prudence stopped me from going closer to her; also, from where I was, I could admire her to the full. She was using every weapon of her charm – her grace, her voice – in the service of her rejected passion. She had told me truthfully; 'You are not the first,' because, in this case, truth struck home more shrewdly than a lie. Her frankness, I could swear, had been calculated, but she loved me!

I was dreaming of her, with her standing there before me, feasting my eyes on the sight of her. A movement in her neck conjured up the familiar Rézi, half-naked, at her dressing-table . . . I gave a sudden shiver, it would be wise not to see her again like that . . .

Irritated and exhausted by my silence, she strained her eyes into the shadow, trying to make out mine.

'Rézi . . .' (I spoke with a great effort) . . . 'please . . . let us give ourselves a rest today from all this and just wait for tomorrow to come . . . tomorrow that straightens out so many tangles! It isn't that you've made me angry, Rézi. I'd have come yesterday, and I'd have laughed or I'd have scolded, if I weren't so fond of you . . .'

With that alert movement of an animal on the watch, she thrust out her chin, faintly cleft with a vertical dimple.

'. . . You must let me think, Rézi, without enveloping me so much, without casting such a net over me – a net of looks, gestures that come close without actually touching, persistent thoughts . . . You must come and sit over here near me, put your head on my knees and not say anything or move. Because, if you move, I shall go away . . .'

She sat down at my feet, laid her head on my lap with a sigh, and clasped her hands behind my waist. I could not stop my fingers from trembling as I ran them through her lovely hair, combing it into ringlets whose gleam was the only brightness left in the dark room. She did not stir. But her scent rose up from the nape of her neck, her burning cheeks warmed me and, against my knees, I could feel the shape of her breasts . . . I was terrified lest she should move. For, had she seen my face and how profoundly disturbed I was . . .

But she did not move, and, this time, too, I was able to leave her without admitting my disturbance, so painfully like her own.

Out in the sharp, cold air, I calmed my jangled nerves as best I could. In situations of that kind, one's still undamaged 'self-esteem' is definitely supposed to brace one up, isn't it? Well, all I can say personally is that I felt I had been rather a mug.

Today, I wager that the people who appear regularly on my husband's 'day' must have said to themselves as they left the house, 'Why, she's getting quite sociable, that little wife of Renaud's! She's becoming civilized!'

No, good people, I am not becoming civilized. I was sociable simply because I was in a daze. That woolly affability, those feverish hands that were a menace to teacups, were not for you! It was not you, old gentleman addicted to

Greek literature and Russian vodka, whom I waited on with the zeal of a young Hebe! That unconscious smile with which I greeted your proposal to visit me in my own home (like the manicurist) to read Pierre Leroux to me was not for you, novelist with socialist pretensions and a sharp eye to the main chance! Nor, Andalusian sculptor, was the earnest expression with which I followed your flood of Hispano-French invectives against contemporary art: my passionate attention was registering not only your aesthetic axioms ('All men of talent, he is dead seence two centuries'), but listening to Rézi's laugh – Rézi, in a close-fitting sheath of white cloth, the same dull, creamy white as her flowing *crêpe-de-Chine* négligé. Andalusian sculptor, you must have renounced all hope of my aversion when I said: 'I've seen the Rubenses' – Ah! And what do you think?' – 'They're tripe!' How feeble the word 'swine' seemed to you and how you wished I'd fall dead at your feet!

Nevertheless, I am still alive, and I am living in the most revolting respectability. The violence of Rézi's attraction, the vanity of my resistance, the sense that I am behaving ridiculously, all urge me to get it over and done with; to intoxicate myself with her till I have exhausted her charm. But, to make a wretched pun, I rézist! And I despise myself for my own stubborn obstinacy.

Today again, she went off with the chattering throng of men who had been smoking and drinking and women who were a little tipsy from the extreme heat of the room, after the cold outside. She went off, kept well in sight by her husband without my having told her: 'I love you . . . I'll see you tomorrow.' Went proudly, the wretch, as if she were sure of me in spite of myself; sure of herself, menacing and passionate . . .

When Renaud and I were left alone at last, we gazed at each other dejectedly, like weary victors on a battlefield. He yawned, opened a window, and leant his elbow on the sill. I went and stood beside him to drink in the cool misty air, the clean wind, damp from a shower. The feel of his great arm round me soon turned my thoughts from the path they were pursuing, now racing in a confused rush, now trailing along, broken, like shreds of clouds.

I wished that Renaud, who stands a head and shoulders

higher than myself, were even taller still. I wanted to be the daughter, or the wife, of a giant Renaud so that I could nestle into the hollow of his elbow, inside the cavern of his sleeve . . . Snug in the shelter of his ear, he would carry me away over endless plains, through enormous forests and, when the storm raged, his hair would moan in the wind like a pine-tree . . .

But Renaud (the real one not the giant) made a movement and, at that, my fairy-tale took fright and vanished . . .

'Claudine,' he said in his full voice, velvety as his eyes. 'I rather think you've made it up, you and Rézi. Am I right?'

'It depends on whether I'm willing to . . . I'm letting her do all the pleading.'

'No harm in that, Claudine, no harm in that! And is she still crazy about you?'

'She is. But I'm still keeping her languishing after . . . after my forgiveness. "The greater the labour."'

'"The greater the prize,"' he chanted in an operatic baritone. 'She looked very pretty today, your friend!'

'I've never seen her look anything but pretty.'

'I believe you. Is the small of her back attractive?'

I was thoroughly startled.

'The small of her back? Why, I haven't the faintest idea! Do you imagine she receives me in her bath?'

'Why, yes. I did imagine so.'

I shrugged my shoulders.

'It's unworthy of you, setting little traps like that! You might believe that I'm sufficiently honest and sufficiently fond of you . . . Renaud, to own up to you frankly, when the day comes: "I've let Rézi go further than I meant to . . ."'

The arm that encircled my shoulders turned me round to face the lighted room.

'Will you, Claudine?'

His face was bent down over mine; on it I could read curiosity and eagerness, but not a trace of anxiety.

'So in fact you can see it coming, the day when you'll have to own up?'

'That isn't what I've got to tell you tonight,' I said, averting my eyes.

I was being evasive, because I felt more tremulously

agitated than a little moth, one of those little reddish moths with phosphorescent eyes that flutter over asters and flowering laurels. When you hold one in your hand, you can feel its velvet body breathing and suffocating as you linger over its poignant warmth . . .

Tonight, all my self-possession has gone. If my husband wants me – and he will – I shall be the Claudine who terrifies him and wildly excites him, the one who flings herself into love-making as if it were for the last time, and who clings, trembling, to Renaud's arm, with no resource against herself . . .

'Renaud, do you think Rézi may be a vicious woman?'

It was nearly two in the morning. In the total darkness, I lay resting huddled close against Renaud's side. He was still in a state of rapture, perfectly ready to plunge me back into the dizzy vortex from which I had just surfaced; I could hear his hurried, irregular heartbeats beneath my head . . . Querulous and shattered, with my bones turned to water, I was enjoying the convalescence that follows moments of too fierce intensity . . . but, along with sanity, I had recovered the obsession that never leaves me, and, with it, the image of Rézi.

Whether I see her – a white figure with outstretched arms swathed in her long dress – lighting up the darkness where coloured specks dance before my exhausted eyes; whether she is sitting, absorbed, at her dressing-table, her arms raised and her face hidden, so that all I see is the nape whose amber melts into the pale gold of the hairline, it is Rézi, always Rézi. Now that she is no longer there, I am not sure that she loves me. My faith in her is limited to an exasperated desire for her presence.

'Renaud, do you think she may be vicious?'

'My sweet lunatic child, I've told you that, as far as I know, Madame Lambrook hasn't any lovers.'

'That's not what I'm asking you. Having lovers doesn't mean a person's vicious.'

'No? Then what do you understand by vice? Homosexuality?'

'Yes and no. It depends how it's practised. But that still isn't vice.'

93

'I'm longing to hear your definition! It must be something quite out of the ordinary.'

'Then I'm afraid you're going to be disappointed. Because, after all, it's self-evident. I take a lover . . .'

'Do you, indeed?'

'It's a supposition.'

'A supposition for which you'll get your bottom smacked if you don't look out!'

'I take a lover, without loving him, simply because I know it's wrong: *that's* vice. I take a lover . . .'

'That makes two.'

'. . . a lover whom I love or whom I simply desire – keep still, Renaud, will you? – that's just obeying the law of nature and I consider myself the most innocent of creatures. To sum up, vice is doing wrong without enjoying it . . .'

'Let's talk about something else, shall we? All these lovers you've taken . . . I need to purify you . . .'

'All right, purify me, then.'

All the same, if I had talked of taking 'a girl-friend' instead of 'a lover' he would have thought my little bit of reasoning eminently sound. For Renaud, adultery is a question of sex.

She makes me uneasy. In her artful gentleness, her shrewd avoidance of anything that might arouse my mistrust, I can no longer recognize the pale, passionate Rézi who beseeched me in a fever of tears . . . But a glance, bright with mischief and loving defiance, has revealed the secret of all this discretion: she knows that I . . . love her – I wish there were a less crude word, a word that conveyed subtler shades of meaning. She has noticed my confusion at being left alone with her; when we exchange a brief kiss at meeting and parting (I daren't avoid kissing her altogether!), she must feel me tremble, as she does herself. She knows now, and she is waiting. Commonplace tactics, if you like. A lover's trap, as old as love itself, yet, forewarned as I am, I dread falling into it. Oh, calculating Rézi! I was able to resist your desire, but can I resist my own?

'Giving oneself up to the intoxication of cherishing and desiring, forgetting everything one has loved before, beginning to love all over again, being rejuvenated by the freshness of a new conquest – that's what makes life supremely worth living! . . .'

It was not Rézi who spoke thus. It was not myself. It was Marcel! His perversity has attained a certain grandeur now that the excitement of a new passion is heightening his tired beauty and his flowering romanticism.

Sitting opposite me, slumped in a big armchair, he was talking like someone in delirium, his eyes lowered, his knees together. And all the time he kept making a compulsive maniacal little gesture, stroking his eyebrows that were pencilled to lengthen their curve.

He certainly has no love for me, but I have never jeered at his peculiar affairs, and perhaps that is why he confides in me.

I listened to him seriously, and not unperturbed. 'Giving oneself up to the intoxication of cherishing and desiring, forgetting everything that one loved . . .'

'Marcel, why must one forget?'

He raised his chin in token of ignorance.

'Why? I don't know. I forget, in spite of myself. Yesterday turns pale and misty behind today.'

'Personally, I'd prefer to bury Yesterday and its withered flowers in the fragment casket of my memory.'

Almost unconsciously, I was imitating his metaphorical redundancy.

'I can't argue about it,' he said, dismissing it with a careless gesture. 'Anyway, give me news of your Today and her rather sensual Viennese charm.'

I frowned and lowered my head in a threatening way.

'Gossip busy already, Marcel?'

'No. Only intuition. After all, I've had so much practice! . . . Besides, you so *definitely* prefer blondes!'

'Why the plural?'

'Aha! Rézi's got you on a string now, but there was a time when you didn't find *me* unattractive!'

What cheek! His spoilt vanity is mistaken. Ten months ago, I would have slapped him; but at this moment I wonder whether I am any better than he. All the same! I stared at him from quite close to, fastening my eyes on his frail temples that would soon shrivel, on the tired crease that already marked his lower lid. And, having ruthlessly scrutinized him, I announced spitefully:

'Marcel, when you're thirty, you'll look like a little old woman.'

So he had noticed it! So it was visible, then? I dared not reassure myself by admitting that Marcel had a special flair. The lazy and fatalistic passion that guided me whispered this advice: 'Since people believe it so, it might just as well be so!'

It was easy enough to say! If Rézi continues to woo me silently with her presence and her glances, at least she seems to have renounced any effective attack. She adorns her beauty in front of me like someone polishing a weapon, incenses me with her fragrance and mockingly flaunts all her perfections at me. She puts an audacious childish mischievousness into the game, but plays fair as regards her gestures so that I cannot complain.

'Claudine, look at my toe-nails! I've got a marvellous new nail-powder. My nails are little convex mirrors . . .'

The slender foot kicked off the mule and rose up, brazen and naked, displaying the gleaming, deliciously artificial pink of the nails that tipped the pale toes . . . then at the very moment when I might have been about to seize it and kiss it, it vanished.

There is also the temptation of the hair; Rézi lazily entrusts me with the task of combing it. I acquit myself brilliantly, especially at the beginning. But prolonged contact with this golden stuff that I unravel and that is so electric that it clings to my dress and crackles under the tortoiseshell comb, like burning bracken, is too much for me. The magic of that intoxicating hair penetrates all through me and makes me torpid . . . Weakly, I let fall the loosened sheaf and Rézi becomes impatient – or pretends to.

Yesterday night at dinner – a dinner for fifteen at the Lambrooks' – while everyone was busy coping with lobster *à l'américaine*, she even dared to look me full in the face and make the adorable mime of a kiss – a silent, complete kiss, with her lips first pursed, then parted, and her sea-grey eyes open and imperious, then veiled.

I was terrified that someone might see her and even more shaken by seeing her myself.

Sometimes this nerve-racking game embarrasses Rézi herself. This happened this morning, in her flat.

Wearing a straw-coloured petticoat and corsets, she was twisting and undulating in front of the mirrors, trying to do the back-bends like a 'Spanish' dancer in Montmartre and get the nape of her neck on a level with her hips.

'Claudine, can you do that?'

'Yes, and better than you can.'

'I'm sure, dear. You're like a well-tempered foil, hard and supple . . . Ah!'

'What's the matter?'

'Are there mosquitoes at this time of year? Quick, quick. Look at my precious skin I love so much . . . and I've got to wear a low neck tonight!'

She made an effort to see a bite (imaginary?) behind her bare shoulder. I bent forward.

'There, there, a little above the shoulder-blade, higher, yes, that's it . . . something stung me . . . What can you see?'

I could see, close enough to touch, the perfectly curved shoulder, Rézi's anxious profile, and, lower down, two bared young breasts round and far apart, like the ones gallants toy with in naughty eighteenth-century engravings. I saw all this, stupefied, and did not say a word. I was unaware, at first, of the intense gaze she had fixed on me. That gaze attracted mine at last, but I averted it to dwell on the peerless whiteness of that flawless, even-tinted skin where the breasts broke abruptly into pink at the tips, the same pink as her nail-varnish . . .

Triumphant, Rézi followed my wandering eyes. But because they had become fixed and urgent, she weakened herself and her eyelashes fluttered like wasp-wings . . . Her eyes turned bluer and rolled upwards and it was she who whispered, 'No, no . . . *please* . . .' as palpably shaken as I was myself.

'*Please* . . .' That word, breathed on a sigh, with a mixture of sensuality and childishness, has done more to precipitate my defeat than the most searching caress.

97

NINE

'MY DARLING CHILD, whatever time's this you're coming in? When for once we're dining alone at home! . . . Come along, quick; you look perfectly all right as you are; don't rush off to your bedroom on the excuse of tidying up your curls – or we'll be here till midnight! Come along, sit down, sweet! I've ordered something special for you tonight – those revolting aubergines with parmesan that you adore.'

'Yes . . .'

I heard what he said without taking it in. Leaving Renaud holding my hat, I dug my fists into my hair and rubbed my overheated head, then collapsed on to the leather chair opposite my husband, under the kindly, shaded light.

'No soup?'

I wrinkled my nose in disgust.

'Tell me where you've come from, with that sleep-walking expression and those eyes burning holes in your face. From Rézi's, eh?'

'Yes . . .'

'Claudine, my girl, you must admit I'm not a jealous husband!'

Not jealous enough, alas! That was what I ought to have answered, instead of merely being content to think it. But he thrust a swarthy face towards me, barred by a moustache lighter than the skin and softened by a feminine smile. He looked so radiant with amorous fatherliness that I did not dare.

To occupy my restless hands, I broke off some golden

crumbs to convey them to my mouth, but my hand dropped again; the obstinate perfume that clung to it made me go suddenly pale.

'Are you ill, my little one?' Renaud asked anxiously, flinging away his table-napkin . . .

'No, no! Tired, that's all. Please, I'm awfully thirsty . . .'

He rang the bell and asked for the sparkling wine I like, the musty Asti I can never drink without a smile . . . But this time, I was tipsy before I had drunk a drop.

All right, yes, I had come from Rézi's! I wanted to scream, to stretch my arms till the sinews crackled so as to melt the maddening stiffness in the nape of my neck.

I had gone to see her, as I do every day, about five o'clock. Without ever making an appointment, she always faithfully waits in for me then; without having made any promise, I faithfully arrive at that hour.

I go to her on foot, walking fast. I watch the days drawing out and the March showers washing the pavements; the daffodils from Nice, heaped on the little barrows, fill the rainy air with their precocious, intoxicating, vulgar spring.

It is on that short road that I study the march of the seasons now, I who used to watch as alertly as an animal for the first pointed leaf in the wood, the first wild anemone like a glimmer of mauve-streaked white flame, for the first willow catkins, whose little furry tails smelt like honey. Wild creature of the forest, you are caged now and you do not want to escape.

Today, as always, Rézi was waiting for me in her green-and-white bedroom. The bed is painted dull white and the late Louis XV armchairs are upholstered in almond-green silk, scattered with little white bows and big white bunches of flowers. Against this tender green, her skin and her hair look dazzling.

But today . . .

'How dark it is in here, Rézi! And there's no light in the hall! Say something. I can't even see you.'

Her voice answered me sulkily, coming from a deep armchair, one of those wicked chairs that are too wide for one person and a little too narrow for two . . .

99

'Yes; gay, isn't it? Something's gone wrong with the electricity. Apparently they can't fix it till tomorrow morning. Naturally, we've got nothing here to use instead. The maid was actually talking of sticking candles in the bottles on my dressing-table! . . .'

'Well, wouldn't that look rather attractive?'

'Thanks! . . . You always side with evil Fate against me . . . Candles! I'd feel I was lying on my bier! They're too funereal for words. Instead of coming and consoling me, you stand over there all by yourself, laughing. I can hear you laughing! Come and sit with me in the big armchair, Claudine darling . . .'

I did not hesitate for a second. Huddled in the big chair, with my arms around her waist, I could feel her body warm and untrammelled under a loose dress, and her sent rose up in my nostrils.

'Rézi, you're like the white tobacco flower that waits for the dark to release all its scent . . . Once evening comes, you can't smell anything else; it puts the roses to shame.'

'Do I really wait for the dark before I give off my scent?'

She let her head fall on my shoulder. I held her close, feeling her living warmth throbbing under my hands, like a trapped partridge.

'Is your husband going to rise up out of the shadows again like an Anglo-Indian Satan?' I asked in a muffled voice.

'No,' she sighed. 'He's taking some compatriots round Paris.'

'Indians?'

'Englishmen.'

Neither she nor I were paying any attention to what we said. The darkness covered us. I did not dare loosen my arms and besides I did not want to.

'Claudine, I love you . . .'

'Why say it?'

'Why not say it? For your sake, I've given up everything, even the flirtations that were the only thing that relieved my boredom. Can you ask me to be more restrained? Don't I torture myself because I'm afraid of making you angry?'

'Torture yourself? Oh, Rézi . . .'

'It's the only word. It *is* torture to love and desire unappeasably; you know it is.'

Yes, I knew it . . . How well I knew it . . . What was I doing at that moment except delighting in that useless pain?

With an imperceptible movement, she had turned still more towards me, clinging close against me from shoulder to knee. I had hardly felt her move; she seemed to have swivelled round inside her dress.

'Rézi, don't talk to me any more. I'm in a trance of laziness and well-being. Don't force me to get up from here . . . Imagine that it's night and we're travelling . . . Imagine the wind in your hair . . . bend down, that low branch might wet your forehead! . . . Squeeze close against me – mind out, the water in the deep ruts is splashing up under the wheels . . .'

All her supple body followed my game with a treacherous compliance. Her hair, tossed back from the head that lay on my shoulder, brushed against my face like the twigs I had invented to distract me from inner turmoil.

'I'm travelling,' she murmured.

'But shall we arrive?'

Her two hands nervously gripped my free one.

'Yes, Claudine. We shall arrive.'

'Where?'

'Bend down, and I'll whisper it to you.'

Credulously, I obeyed. And it was her mouth that I encountered. I listened for a long time to what her mouth told mine . . . She had not lied; we were arriving . . . My haste equalled her own, then surpassed and outstripped it. In a revelation of self-knowledge, I thrust away Rézi's caressing hands. She understood, trembled all over, struggled for a brief second, then lay back, her arms hanging limp.

The dull thud of a distant street-door brought me to my feet. Rézi's warm lips were pressed to my wrist; all I could make out was the pale blur of her seated figure. With one arm round her waist, I pulled her up and crushed her whole body against me, bending her back, and kissing her at random on her eyes, on her dishevelled hair, on her moist nape . . .

'Tomorrow!'

'Tomorrow . . . I love you.'

101

I ran down the street, with my head buzzing. My fingers still tingled from the slight scratchiness of lace, still seemed to be slithering on the satin of an untied ribbon, still felt the velvet of a peerless skin. And the evening air hurt me like a knife, tearing the veil of perfume she had woven all about me.

'Claudine, if even aubergines with parmesan leave you cold . . . I know where to look for the reason!'

I started at the sound of Renaud's voice; I had been a very long way away. It was true I was not eating. But I was so thirsty!

'Darling, isn't there something you want to tell me?'

This husband of mine is certainly not like other husbands! Vexed by his persistence, I implored him:

'Renaud, don't tease me . . . I'm tired, I'm nervous, I'm embarrassed in front of you . . . Let's get the night over, and for heaven's sake, don't imagine so many things!'

He said no more. But, after dinner, he kept watching the clock and, at half past ten, insisted that he was shockingly sleepy, a thing that he never admits. And, once we were in our great bed, he lost not a moment before seeking in my hair, on my hands, on my mouth the truth I did not want to tell him!

'Tomorrow!' Rézi had implored. 'Tomorrow!' I had consented. Alas! this Tomorrow did not come. I hurried round to her, sure of a longer, more perfectly savoured bliss now that there would be a light again to show me this marvellous, vanquished Rézi . . . But I had completely forgotten her husband! He disturbed us twice, the fiend; twice, by an abrupt entrance, he made our timid hungry hands fly apart! We stared at each other, Rézi and I, she on the verge of tears, I in such a furious rage, that had there been a third intrusion, it would have been all I could do not to throw my glass of orangeade in the face of that stiff, suspicious, polite husband . . . And that throbbing 'Good-bye,' those stolen kisses, those furtive pressures of our fingers are no longer enough to satisfy us now . . .

What can we do?

I came home, alternately building up and sweeping away impossible plans. It was hopeless!

Today I went back to Rézi's flat to tell her of my utter helplessness, to see her, to breathe in her sweetness.

She rushed to meet me, as anxious as I was myself.

'Well, darling?'

'I haven't found any solution. Are you angry with me?'

Her eyes caressed the curve of my mouth as I spoke and her lips trembled and parted . . . I caught the infection of her desire and my whole being was hungry for her. Was I going to seize her then and there in that smug drawing-room and kiss her to death?

She guessed what I was thinking and drew back a step. 'No,' she said in a low, hurried voice, pointing to the door.

'Then in my flat, Rézi?'

'In yours, if you like . . .'

I smiled; then I shook my head.

'No! The bell keeps ringing all the time; Renaud is always in and out; the doors bang . . . Oh, no!'

She wrung her white hands in a little gesture of despair.

'Then it's to be never again? Do you imagine I can live for a month on the memory of yesterday? It ought never to have happened,' she ended, turning away her head. 'If you can't quench my thirst for you every day . . .'

Tenderly sulky, she went over and collapsed in the big armchair, the same one . . . And though today she was sheathed in a tight-fitting wool street-dress, honey-pale as her hair, I recognized only too well the curve of her half-reclining hips and the tapering line of her legs that were silvered with almost invisible velvet down.

'Oh, Rézi!'

'What?'

'The carriage?'

'The carriage? Jolts, starts, cricks in the neck . . . curious faces suddenly glued to the window, a horse falling, a zealous policeman opening the door, the driver discreetly tapping with the handle of his whip: "Madame, the road's blocked. Should I turn back?" No, Claudine, definitely *not* the carriage!'

'Then, my dear, find somewhere possible for us yourself . . . up to now you've found nothing but objections!'

Swift as a snake when you touch it, she reared up her golden head and darted me looks full of tearful reproach.

'Is that all your love amounts to? You wouldn't dream of being offended if you loved me as much as I love you!'

I shrugged my shoulders.

'Then why keep putting up all these barriers? The carriage paralyses you, this drawing-room bristles with matrimonial traps . . . have we got to take in the Saturday *Journal* and look for a shelter you hire by the day?'

'I'd do that gladly,' she sighed ingenuously, 'but all those places are watched by the police so . . . so somebody told me.'

'I don't care a fig about the police.'

'*You* don't have to, thanks to the sort of husband you have, thanks to Renaud . . .'

Her voice changed.

'Claudine,' she said slowly and thoughtfully, 'Renaud – Renaud's the only person who can . . .'

I stared at her, dumbfounded, without finding any reply. She was thinking very earnestly, sitting there, slim in her honey-coloured dress, her fists under her childish chin.

'Yes, Claudine, our peace of mind depends on him . . . and on you.'

She held out her arms, and her impenetrable, tender face appealed to me.

'Our peace of mind, oh! my dear, our happiness, call it what you like. Only realize that I can't bear to wait, now that I have felt your strength, now that Rézi is yours, with all her passion and all her weakness!'

I slipped into her arms, and bent over her lips, prepared to resign myself to tight, hampering garments, prepared to ruin our delight by over-haste.

She wrenched herself out of my hands: 'Sshh! I heard footsteps.'

How terrified she was! Her whiteness had gone whiter still; she was listening, bending forward, her pupils dilated . . . Oh, if only a chimney would fall and flatten out that accursed Lambrook and deliver us from him!

'Rézi, my golden, why do you think that Renaud . . .?'

'Yes, Renaud! *He's* an intelligent husband and he adores

104

you. You must tell him . . . well, almost everything. He's so fond of you and so clever, he must arrange a "hide-out" for us.'

'You aren't afraid of *my* husband being jealous?'

'No.'

Curious, that little smile of hers! . . . A crazy confidence in her had been growing almost as fast as my desires, why did she have to check it by an ambiguous gesture, a sly inflexion of the mouth? But it was the merest shadow, and if I were to have no more of her than her sincere sensuality, the double softness of her skin and her voice, her glorious hair and her enthralling mouth . . . was not that more than enough? Whatever it cost me, I would ask help – not now, a little later, I wanted to go on searching on my own! – I would ask help from Renaud. For her sake, I would humble my fierce modesty and the loving pride I should have put into discovering a safe haven for our passion entirely on my own.

Enervating sulks, angry tears, tender reconciliations, electric hours when the mere contact of our hands maddened us . . . that is the summary of this last week. I haven't spoken to Renaud. It would cost me so much to do that! And Rézi is resentful because I haven't. I haven't even admitted to my dear giant that Rézi's feeling for me and mine for Rézi is becoming clearer than words can say . . . But he knows almost everything, apart from details, and this certainly induces a strange fever in him. What fantastic, loving panderism leads him to keep urging me to go and see Rézi, to make sure I look my best for her? At four o'clock, when I throw down the book with which I was cheating the time of waiting, Renaud gets up, if he is in the room, and becomes agitated: 'You're going over there? – Yes?' He runs his deft fingers through my hair to fluff up my curls, bends his great moustache down close to me to re-knot my thick knitted silk tie and verify the spotlessness of my boyish collar. Standing behind me, he makes sure that my fur turban is firm and straight, then holds out the sleeves of my sable coat . . . And, finally, it is he who slips into my dazed hands a bunch of dark, red, almost black roses, my friend's favourite flower! I admit that I would never have thought of that!

105

And then comes a big, affectionate kiss.

'Run along, my little girl. Be very good. Be proud, not too humbly loving, make yourself desired . . .'

'Make yourself desired . . .' I am desired, alas! . . . but not as a result of my strategy.

TEN

WHEN IT IS Rézi who comes to see me, the strain on my nerves is even worse. There she is in my bedroom – which is simply *our* bedroom, Renaud's and mine – one turn of the key and we should be alone . . . But I don't want to lock us in. Above all I hate the idea of my husband's maid (a taciturn girl with a silent tread who sews such slack stitches with her flabby hands) knocking and exclaiming in a hushed voice through the closed door: 'It's Madame's blouse . . . I want it to repair the armholes.' I dread the spying of Ernest the manservant with a face like a bad priest's. Those servants of his don't belong to me; I employ them with caution and repugnance. To tell the whole truth, there is something I dread even more – Renaud's curiosity . . .

And that is why all I let Rézi do in my bedroom is weave her most seductive spirals and put on every shade of reproachful expression.

'You haven't found anything for us, Claudine?'

'No.'

'You haven't asked Renaud yet?'

'No.'

'It's cruel . . .'

At that word, sighed almost in a whisper, with her eyes suddenly lowered, I felt my will collapse. But Renaud came and knocked with little cautious taps and received a 'Come in' ruder than a brick in his face, in reply.

I don't at all like the suppliant charm Rézi puts on with Renaud, nor that way he has of trying to find out what we are

107

hiding from him by sniffing at her hair and her dress as if to detect the fragrance left by my kisses.

He did it again today, in front of me . . . He kissed both her hands when he came in, for the pleasure of saying:

'So you've taken to using Claudine's scent, that sweet, dusky Chypre?'

'Why, no,' she replied innocently.

'Funny, I thought you had.'

Renaud switched his gaze on me with a knowing, flattering look. My whole soul flared up with rage. I was so exasperated, I wondered should I tug the ends of his big moustache with all my might till he screamed, till he beat me? . . . No. I managed to contain myself; I preserved the stiff, correct calm of a husband whose wife is being kissed during some innocent party game. To make matters even worse, he was about to make his exit with the insulting discretion of a waiter serving a couple in a private room. I stopped him:

'Do stay, Renaud . . .'

'Not on your life! Rézi would tear my eyes out.'

'Why?'

'My little curly shepherd, I know only too well how precious a *tête-à-tête* with you is.'

An ugly fear poisoned me: suppose Rézi, with her fluctuating, untruthful nature, took to preferring Renaud! He was particularly handsome today, in a long jacket that suited him and drew attention to his broad shoulders and small feet . . . And there was that Rézi, the source of all my trouble, furred in nutria the colour of rye and wearing a prematurely summery hat of lilacs and green leaves . . . I was aware of an old feeling surging up in me again, the brutality that had made me beat and scratch Luce . . . How poignantly sweet Rézi's tears would be to my torment!

She looked at me in silence, putting all her words into her eyes . . . I was going to yield . . . I yielded.

'Renaud, dear, are you going out before dinner?'

'No, little girl, why?'

'I want to talk to you . . . to ask you to do something for me.'

Rézi sprang up from her chair and settled her hat, all gaiety and confusion . . . she had understood.

'I must fly . . . Yes, literally, I can't stay another moment . . . But tomorrow I'll see you for a long time, Claudine. Ah! Renaud, how one ought to envy you this child of yours!'

She disappeared with the rustling of her dress, leaving Renaud confounded.

'She's mad, I take it? Whatever's come over the two of you?'

Oh, heavens! Could I really say it? How hard it was! . . .

'Renaud . . . I . . . you . . .'

'What is it, little one? You've gone all pale!'

He drew me on his knees. Perhaps it would be easier there . . .

'The fact is . . . Rézi's husband's an awful nuisance.'

'He certainly is . . . especially to her!'

'To me too.'

'The devil he is! . . . You mean he's had the impertinence to try something on?'

'No. Don't move; keep me in your arms. Only this wretched Lambrook is always on our backs.'

'Ah! I see.'

Of course, I ought to know by now that Renaud is anything but a fool. He understands at the first hint.

'My dear little amorous pussy-cat! So you're being tormented, you and your Rézi? What's to be done about it. You're quite aware that your old husband loves you enough not to deprive you of a little pleasure . . . She's charming, your fair-haired friend. She loves you so tremendously!'

'Does she? Do you really think so?'

'I'm certain of it! And you two beauties complement each other. Your amber can hold its own against her dazzling whiteness . . .'

His arms had trembled . . . I knew what he was imagining. Nevertheless I relaxed at the sound of his voice; overflowing with tenderness, genuine tenderness.

'What do you want me to do, my darling bird? Leave this flat empty the whole of the afternoon?'

'Oh! no . . .'

I added, after an embarrassed silence:

109

'. . . If we could . . . somewhere else . . .'

'Somewhere else? Why, nothing easier!'

He rose to his feet with one bound, set me on the floor and walked up and down with long, very youthful strides . . .

'Somewhere else . . . let's see . . . of course there's . . . No, not that – it's not good enough . . . Ah! I've got the very thing for you!'

He came back to me, flung his arms round me and searched for my mouth. But, quite frigid with confusion and shyness, I turned slightly away . . .

'My charming little girl, you shall have your Rézi. Rézi shall have her Claudine. Don't worry about anything any more . . . except having to be patient for one day . . . two days at the most . . . That's not long, is it? Kiss your faithful giant who will be blind and deaf as he keeps guard over the threshold of your room and those soft whisperings inside . . .'

The joy, the certainty of possessing Rézi in all the glory of her scented whiteness, the relief of having confessed the ugly secret, did not prevent me from feeling another kind of unhappiness. Oh, dear Renaud, how I would have loved you for a sharp, scolding refusal!

I had hoped that night of waiting would be happy, alternating between flutters of sweet apprehension and half-waking dreams through which Rézi drifted in a haze of golden light . . . But the very fact that I was waiting conjured up another vigil in my little bedroom in the rue Jacob. That had been a younger, more fierily impetuous Claudine . . . Would Rézi find me beautiful enough? Ardent enough, oh yes, I was sure of that . . . Weary of lying awake, I put out a slim cold foot to disturb Renaud's light sleep so that I could huddle my body, prickling all over with nerves, in the shelter of his arm. And there, at last, I dozed off.

Dreams succeeded each other and melted into each other in a tangled, confused blur, impossible to analyse: sometimes a young, supple figure would appear in the fog, then vanish, like the moon shining through clouds, then veiled again . . . When I called 'Rézi,' she turned round, showing me the gentle, rounded forehead, the velvety eyelids and full, short lips of little black-and-white Hélène. What was she doing in my

110

dreams, that schoolgirl, glimpsed for a moment and very nearly forgotten?

Renaud wasted no time. He arrived home for dinner last night excited, boisterous and demonstrative.

'Tell Hélène to prepare!' he said as he kissed me. 'Bid that young witch wash and anoint herself for tomorrow's Sabbath!'

'Tomorrow? Where?'

'You'll know in due course! Tell her to meet us here; I'll take you both with me. It's not good for you to be seen going in by yourselves. And, besides, I'll see you comfortably settled in.'

This arrangement chilled me a little: I would have liked the key, the address of the room, freedom . . .

Rézi arrived before the appointed time, looking anxious. Making an attempt to laugh, I said to her:

'Will you come with me? Renaud has found us a . . . a "bachelor-girls' flat".'

Her eyes danced and a golden glint came into them.

'Ah! . . . So he knows that I know that he . . .'

'Of course! How else would it have been possible? You yourself suggested . . . and I'm thankful now, that you were so persistent, Rézi . . . my asking Renaud's help . . .'

'Yes, yes. I did . . .'

Her sly, caressing grey eyes became anxious and sought mine; her hand went up to her hair and kept circling round and round as she tucked in stray gold wisps on her nape.

'I'm afraid you don't love me enough, today, not enough for . . . that, Claudine!'

Her mouth was too close as she said it; I could feel her breath and that was enough to make me clench my jaws and bring the blood to my ears . . .

'I always love you enough . . . too much . . . madly, Rézi . . . Yes, I would far rather that no one in the world had authorized us or forbidden us to have an afternoon alone together, safe behind a locked door. But if in that room, wherever it is, whoever found it, I can believe for one moment that you belong to me, that I am the only one . . . I shall regret nothing.'

She listened to the sound of my voice as if in a daydream; perhaps she did not even hear the words. When Renaud entered, we started simultaneously and, for a minute, Rézi lost a little of her self-assurance. He dissipated her embarrassment with a kindly, conspiratorial laugh, then, looking mysterious, produced a small key from his waistcoat pocket.

'Hist! To whom shall I entrust it?'

'To me,' I said, holding out an imperious hand.

'To me!' Rézi implored coaxingly.

'*How happy could I be with either*,' warbled Renaud, '*were t'other dear charmer away.*'

At this Maugis-like joke, and the shrill laugh with which Rézi greeted it, I felt on the verge of a clumsy outburst of rage. Did Renaud divine this? He stood up:

'Come along, children. The carriage is down below.'

Sitting opposite us on the penitential, pull-down seat, he could hardly disguise his excitement over this escapade. His nose whitened and his moustache quivered when his eyes wandered over Rézi. The latter tried, uncertainly, to make conversation, gave it up and looked inquiringly at me in my sad, haughty impatience . . .

Yes, I was eaten up with impatience! Impatience to savour all that Rézi's urgency had promised me during this week of stress and strain; impatience above all to arrive, to end this shocking expedition as a threesome.

What? We were stopping in the rue Goethe? So near home? It seemed to me that we had been driving for half an hour . . . The staircase of number 59 wasn't bad. There were stables at the bottom of the courtyard. Two storeys. Renaud opened a noiseless door and, the moment one entered the hall, one was conscious of the thick, heavy air of rooms hung with material.

While I was examining the little drawing-room with a slightly hostile eye, Rézi ran to the window and, in a prudent (I don't want to write 'experienced') way, inspected the outside without raising the white net curtains. Presumably satisfied, she wandered, like myself, about the minute drawing-room, where an amateur of Louis XIII Spanish furniture had indulged his mania to the full. It was crammed with carved and gilded wood, heavy ornamental frames, crucifixes on moth-eaten velvet, hostile *prie-dieus* and an enormous sedan chair, ponderous and splendid, with a cornucopia of autumn fruits, apples, grapes, and pears, carved in full relief on its sides . . . This sacrilegious austerity pleased me and I relaxed my frown. A half-drawn curtain in the doorway revealed the corner of a light, English-style bedroom, the knob of a brass bedstead and a pleasant couch covered with flowered material . . .

'I like the look of it. Definitely.'

'Renaud, it's charming!' declared Rézi. 'Whose place is this?'

'Yours, fair Bilitis! Here's the electric light switch. Here's some tea and some lemon, here are some black grapes, and, lastly, here is my heart that throbs for both of you . . .'

How utterly at ease he was and with what good grace he fulfilled his dubious role! I watched him bustling about, arranging the saucers with his deft, feminine hands, smiling with his blue-black eyes, holding out a bunch of grapes to Rézi that she nibbled coquettishly . . . Why was I astonished at his behaviour when he was not astonished at mine?

. . . I was holding her against my heart, against the whole length of my body. Her cool knees touched me, her little toe-nails scratched me deliciously. Her crumpled chemise was nothing but a rag of muslin. My bent arm supported the precious weight of her neck, her face was half-buried in the torrent of her hair. The day was ending, the shadow was dimming the bright leaves on the hangings whose unfamiliarity galled me. Rézi's mouth was very close to mine; from time to time a glint of light, like a sun-gleam on a river, shone on her teeth as she talked. She talked in a fever of gaiety, one bare arm raised and her forefinger drawing what she said. In the twilight, I followed that white and sinuous arm whose gestures made a rhythmic accompaniment to my languor and the adorable sadness that drugged me . . .

I wanted her to be sad, as I was; I wanted her to be quiet and fearful at the thought of the minutes flying past; I wanted her, at least, to leave me to brood on my memory . . .

As if the caress had wounded her, she had turned a

marvellous animal face towards me; eyebrows lowered, upper lip raised and snarling, an expression of frenzy and supplication . . . Then everything melted into wild surrender, into murmuring, imperious demands, into a kind of amorous fury, followed by childish 'Thank-yous' and great, satisfied sighs of 'Ah!' like a little girl who had been dreadfully thirsty and drunk everything down at a gulp, leaving her out of breath . . .

Now she was talking, and her voice, dear as it was, disturbed the precious hour . . . She was, in fact, chattering her joy aloud, just like Renaud . . . Couldn't they savour it in silence? There was I, sombre as that unfamiliar bedroom . . . What a bad after-love-making companion I am!

I roused myself to life again by straining close the warm body that adapted itself to mine and flexed when I flexed; the beloved body, so fleshy in its tapering slimness that nowhere could I feel the resisting skeleton beneath . . .

'Ah! Claudine, you crush me so tight in your arms! . . . Yes, I assure you that his frigidity, his outrageous jealousy justify everything.'

She was talking of her husband! I was not listening. And what need had she of excuses? That word rang false here. With a kiss, I dammed the flow of her soft chatter . . . for a few seconds.

'Claudine, I swear no one's ever made me suffer the torture of waiting as *you* have. So many weeks wasted, my love! Think, it'll soon be spring and every day is bringing us nearer the summer holidays that will separate us . . .'

'I forbid you to go away!'

'Yes, do forbid me something!' she implored, invincibly tender, clinging to me. 'Scold me, don't leave me, I don't want to see anyone but you . . . and Renaud.'

'Ah! So Renaud finds favour with you?'

'Yes, because he's kind, because he's got the soul of a woman, because he understands us and protects our privacy . . . Claudine, I don't feel ashamed in front of Renaud. Isn't that odd?'

Odd indeed, and I envy Rézi. For *I* am ashamed. No, that's not quite the right word . . . What I am rather is . . . a little . . . scandalized. That's it. My husband shocks me.

114

'. . . And, in my case, darling,' she wound up, raising herself on one elbow, 'the three of us are involved in a little adventure that's far from commonplace!'

'Far from commonplace! A little adventure!' That babbler! If I kissed her mouth rather cruelly, didn't she guess why? I wanted to bite off her pointed tongue; I wanted to love the mute, docile Rézi, perfect in her silence, eloquent only in look and gesture.

I annihilated myself in my kiss, aware only of her quick, fluttering breath fanning my nostrils . . . It had grown dark but I cupped Rézi's head in my two hands like a fruit, ruffling her hair that was so fine that I could have guessed its colour merely by the feel of it . . .

'Claudine, I'm sure it's seven o'clock.'

She leapt out of bed, rushed over to the switch and flooded us with light.

Left solitary and chilly, I curled up in the warm place where she had lain to keep the heat of her body a little longer, to permeate myself with the smell of her blonde skin. *I* had plenty of time. My husband was not anxiously expecting me home . . . quite the reverse!

Dazed by the light, she spun round for a moment, unable to find her scattered underclothes. She bent down to pick up a stray tortoiseshell hairpin, stood up again and her chemise slid to the ground. Unembarrassed, she coiled up her hair again, with that swift, deft grace that amuses and charms me . . . The frizz of gold in the hollow of the raised arms and at the base of the youthful stomach was so pale that, in the light, my Rézi seemed as naked as a statue. But what statue would dare display those full, resilient buttocks, so bold and assertive after the slimness of the torso?

Looking very serious, with her hair as irreproachably done as if she were going to a formal party, Rézi pinned her spring-like hat on her head and stood for a moment admiring herself in the glass, arrayed only in a toque of lilac-blossom. I laughed and thereby unfortunately spurred her to hurry. The next moment, the corset, the diaphanous knickers, the dawn-pink petticoat flung themselves on her, undoubtedly summoned by three magic words. Another minute, and the

115

fashionable, sophisticated Rézi stood before me, furred in nutria, gloved in ivory suede, proud of her conjurer's dexterity.

'My blonde girl, it's dark now that all your white and gold doesn't shine brighter than the light . . . Help me to get up. I'm too weak to battle with these sheets that hold me down . . .'

On my feet, stretching up my damp hands to ease the stiff little ache between my shoulder-blades, I studied myself in the huge well-placed mirror. I was proud of my muscular tallness, of my slender grace, more boyish and clear-cut than Rézi's . . .

The nape of her neck slid caressingly under my raised arm and I turned away from the two figures, one dressed, one naked, that the mirror reflected back.

I hurried into my clothes, helped by Rézi. Close to me, she gave off a smell of love-warmed flesh and of fur . . .

'Rézi dear, don't try to teach me your magical speed! Compared to your fairy hands, I shall always look like someone dressing themselves with their feet! What, aren't we going to have any tea?'

'We haven't time,' demurred Rézi, smiling at me.

'Just some black grapes at least? I'm so thirsty . . .'

'All right, some black grapes . . . Come and take them.'

I took them from between her lips, crushing out their juice in my parched mouth . . . I was staggering with exhaustion and desire. She escaped my arms.

The lights were switched off, the door stood ajar on the cold, bright echoing staircase. Rézi, all warm and glowing, offered me her mouth, that tasted of black grapes, for the last time . . . And suddenly I was in the street, being elbowed by passers-by, and because of that unnatural getting dressed again, feeling shivery and faintly sick, as if I had had to get up in the middle of the night.

'Darling child, come here and I'll make you laugh!'

It was Renaud who had come into the dressing-room and interrupted the prolonged morning curry-combing of my short hair. Wedged in the wicker armchair, he was already laughing himself.

'Listen! A devoted female who's willing to keep the rue

Goethe tidy for sixty centimes an hour returned an object (found in the storm-tossed sheets) to me this morning, neatly folded in a scrap of the *Petit Parisien*, with the sole comment: "It's Monsieur's chin-strap".'

'!!! . . .'

'There! You'll promptly get the most unseemly ideas into your head! Look!'

At the end of his fingers dangled a narrow rag of minutely-pleated linen, edged with Malines lace . . . The shoulder-strap of Rézi's chemise! . . . I snatched it from him in mid-air . . . I shan't give it back to him.

'What's more, I suspect that concierge of providing "gags" for our most popular music-hall comedians. Yesterday, about six, I went round there – very discreet – and a trifle anxious about my darling, who was so long coming home – to ask for news of you. She replied, full of respectful censure, "Those two ladies have been waiting nearly two whole hours for Monsieur".'

'So then?'

'So then . . . I didn't come up, Claudine. Kiss me as a reward for that.'

Eleven

THIS WILL NO longer really be Claudine's diary any more, because in it I can talk of nothing but Rézi. What has happened to the old, quick-witted Claudine? She is nothing but a fevered, unhappy creature drifting weakly in Rézi's wake. The days go past without incident, except for our meetings once or twice a week in the rue Goethe. The rest of the time I follow Renaud as he performs his various duties: first nights, dinners, literary parties. I often take my mistress to the theatre, accompanied by Lambrook, just for the craven assurance that at least during those hours she cannot deceive me. I suffer from jealousy and yet . . . I do not love her.

No, I do not love her! But I cannot deprive myself of her, and in any case I do not try to. Away from her, I can imagine, without a tremor, her being knocked down by a motor car or killed in a railway accident. But I cannot, without my ears buzzing and my heart accelerating, say to myself: 'At this very moment she is yielding her mouth to a lover, man or woman, with that hurried flutter of the lashes, that backward tilt of the head as if she were drinking, that I know so well.'

What does it matter that I do not love her, I suffer as much as if I did!

I find it hard to endure Renaud's presence, his all-too-readiness to be involved as a third. He has refused to give me the key of the little flat, alleging, no doubt with good reason, that we must not be seen going into it alone together. And each time it means the same humiliating effort for me to say to him: 'Renaud, tomorrow we're going *over there* . . .'

He always consents eagerly; he is invariably charming – rejoicing, no doubt, like Rézi in the 'far from commonplace' situation . . . That need, common to both of them, to proclaim themselves vicious and ultra-modern, disconcerts me. Yet I do what Rézi does – and even more – and I do not feel I am vicious . . .

Nowadays, Renaud lingers when he accompanies us *over there*. He pours out the tea, sits down, smokes a cigarette, chats, gets up to straighten a picture-frame or flick a moth off the velvet of a *prie-dieu* . . . he makes it obvious that he is at home. And when he finally makes up his mind to go, pretending to apologize for staying so long, it is Rézi who protests, 'Oh, don't go yet . . . do stay another minute . . .' But *I* say nothing.

Their conversation leaves me out of it: gossip, back-biting, jokes that quickly turn bawdy, thinly veiled allusions to what will happen when he has gone . . . She laughs, she plays up to all this boring drivel, exerting the charm of her soft myopic gaze, of those supple twists in her neck and waist . . . I swear, yes, I swear I am so shocked by it all that I feel as embarrassed and outraged as a decent girl confronted with obscene pictures . . . Sensual delight – my form of it – has nothing to do with cosy, giggling 'fun and games'.

In the bright bedroom, where Renaud's Iris and Claudine's harsh sweet Chypre mingle in the air, in the great bed that is fragrant with our two bodies, I avenge myself silently for many a hidden, bleeding wound . . . Afterwards, curled up against me in an attitude blessedly familiar now, Rézi talks and questions me. She is irritated by the brevity and simplicity of my answers, avid to know more, incredulous when I assure her of my former virtue and the novelty of this madness of mine.

'But, after all, what about Luce?'

'Luce? All right, she loved me.'

'And . . . nothing happened?'

'Nothing! Do you think I'm ridiculous?'

'Of course not, my Claudine.'

With her cheek on my breast, she seemed to be listening to some inner voice of her own. Memories brought sparkles into her grey eyes . . . If she spoke, I knew I should want to hit her, yet I longed for her to talk . . .

'Rézi, you didn't wait till you were married?'

'Oh, yes I did!' she cried, sitting up, yielding to the impulse of telling me about herself. 'The beginning couldn't have been more ridiculous, more utterly commonplace . . . My singing-mistress, a peroxide blonde with bones like a horse. Because she had sea-green eyes, she affected arty clothes and a sphinx-like personality. An Anglo-Saxon sphinx! . . . With her, I didn't merely increase my vocal range. I learnt to use the whole gamut of perversity . . . I was very young, newly-married, frightened and a little swept off my feet by her . . . I stopped the lessons at the end of the month – yes, exactly a month – appallingly disillusioned because of a little scene I'd witnessed through a half-open door. The sphinx, swathed in Liberty scarves, was bitterly accusing her cook of having done her out of something less than eighty-five centimes . . .'

Rézi had grown animated; she rocked to and fro, tossing her silky hair and laughing at her comical reminiscence. Sitting, doubled up, in the hollow of my thigh, with one foot in her hand and her chemise slipping off, she seemed to be enjoying herself enormously.

'And, after that, Rézi? Who came next?'

'After that . . . it was . . .'

She hesitated, gave me a swift glance, closed her mouth again, and then made up her mind.

'It was a young girl.'

I could swear, from the way she looked, that she had omitted someone, man or woman.

'A young girl? Really? How interesting!'

I longed to bite her.

'Interesting, yes . . . But I suffered. Oh, never again have I wanted to have anything to do with a young girl!'

Her mouth dropped; sitting there thoughtful and half-naked, she looked like an amorous child. How sharply I would imprint my teeth in two little red curves on that shoulder, pearly in the dimming daylight!

'You . . . loved her, that girl?'

'Yes, I loved her. But now I love no one but you, darling!'

Whether from true fondness or instinctive apprehension, she flung her flawless arms round me and drowned me in the loosened flood of her hair. But I wanted the end of the story . . .

'. . . And she – did she love you?'

'Oh! how can I tell? Claudine, my dearest dear, there's nothing to equal the cruelty, the cold, critical demandingness of young girls! I mean decent young girls; the others don't count. They lack all awareness of suffering, all sense of pity and fairness . . . That one was more ruthless in search of pleasure, more avid than a last year's widow, yet she kept me in suspense for weeks. She'd only see me when her family were there, she would watch my unhappiness with that frank, pretty face and those hard eyes . . . A fortnight later, I learnt the cause of my punishment . . . being five minutes late for a meeting, too lively a conversation with a man friend . . . And the spiteful remarks, the bitter allusions made out loud in public, with the shrill, crude recklessness of girls who haven't yet been softened and scared by their first fall from virtue!'

My pinched and shrunken heart beat faster. I wanted to annihilate the woman who was talking. Nevertheless, I respected her more, carried away into making a truthful admission. I preferred her stormy eyes, darkened by her memory to the childish, provocative gaze she turns on Renaud – and on any man – and on any woman – even on the concierge . . .

Heavens, how changed I am! Not fundamentally changed maybe – I hope not – but . . . disguised. Spring is here, the Paris spring, a little bronchitic, a little tainted, quickly tired, never mind, it *is* spring. And what do I know of it but Rézi's hats? Violets, lilacs, and roses have blossomed in turn on her charming head as if the sunshine of her hair had brought them out. She has presided authoritatively over my sessions with dressmakers and milliners, annoyed to find that certain smart women's hats look so ridiculous on my short, curly hair. She forced me to go along with her to Gauthé's to have myself fitted with this corset-belt of overlapping ribbons, a supple girdle that gives with every movement of my hips. She has fussed busily among materials, picking out the blues that

121

enhance the yellow of my eyes, the strong pinks against which my cheeks look so exotically amber . . . I am dressed by her. I am inhabited by her. I find it hard to resist her. Before I reach her doorstep, I throw away the bunch of wild narcissus, brought from some man in the street. I love their over-rich southern scent, but Rézi does not like it.

Oh, how far I am from being happy! And how can I relieve this anguish that oppresses me? Renaud, Rézi, they are both necessary to me, and there is no question of choosing between them. But how I wish that I could keep them separate, or, better still, that they had never met!

Have I found the remedy? At any rate, it's worth trying.

Marcel came to see me today. He found me in an odd mood, at once gloomy and aggressive. That is because, for the past week, I have been putting off a meeting, though Rézi keeps imploring me, Rézi looking deliciously fresh, excited and stimulated by spring . . . But I can no longer endure Renaud's presence between us. How is it he doesn't sense this? The last time we were at the rue Goethe, my husband's fondly perverse, Peeping Tom mood came up against such savage rudeness that Rézi jumped up anxiously and made him some sign or other . . . He departed at once . . . This kind of understanding between them exasperated me still more. I turned obstinate and, for the first time, Rézi went away without removing the hat that she takes off after her chemise.

So Marcel teased me about my sour expression. He has long ago discovered the secret of my trouble and my joy; he guessed where the sore spot lay with a sureness that would have amazed me had I not known my stepson. Seeing me in a black mood today, he maliciously turned the knife in my little wound.

'Are you a jealous lover?'

'Are you?'

'Me? . . . Yes and no. Do you keep a sharp eye on *her*?'

'What's that got to do with you? Anyway, why *should* I keep an eye on her?'

He shook his delicate, made-up head and lengthily arranged his cravat, shot with changing, iridescent gleams in the hues of a scarab; then he shot me a sidelong glance:

'No reason at all. I hardly know her. It's just a superficial impression *she* gives me – that she's a woman who needs watching.'

I smiled unkindly.

'Really? Your own experiences must make you quite an authority on women . . .'

'Charming,' he conceded, without losing his temper. 'That was a nasty dig. As a matter of fact, you're perfectly right. I saw all three of you at the first night of the Vaudeville. Madame Lambrook looked delicious, I thought maybe that hair-style was a *little* too severe. But what grace! And how obviously she adores you . . . you and my father!'

I controlled myself rigidly and gave no sign. Disappointed, Marcel stood up, with a provocative sway of his hips . . . goodness knows for whose benefit!

'Good-bye. I must get back. You'd depress a writer of gay pornography if they weren't all so dreary already!'

'Who is it you're leaving me for?'

'Myself. I'm on honeymoon with my latest little find.'

'You've got a new . . .?'

'Home, dear, not homo. What, haven't you heard that I'm a free man again?'

'No. *They're* so discreet!'

'Who?'

'Your boy-friends.'

'They have to be. Yes; I've got a little love-nest. But absolutely *minute*! You can just get two in with a tight squeeze.'

'And they do squeeze tight?'

'You said it, not me. Won't you come and see it? By the way, I'd just as soon you didn't bring my dear father. Your girl-friend, if it would amuse her . . . What about it?'

Suddenly, impelled by an idea, I grabbed hold of his wrist.

'You aren't ever out in the afternoon, are you?'

'The afternoon? Yes . . . On Thursdays and Saturdays. But don't imagine,' he added with a charming smile, like a modest girl's, 'that I'm going to tell you where I go.'

'I'm not interested . . . Tell me, Marcel . . . it wouldn't be possible to see it while you were out . . . your little haven of rest?'

'Rest? Hardly that! Except *afterwards*, of course . . .'

He looked at me with a vicious glint in his eyes – blue eyes, shot with sombre grey. He had understood.

'It might be managed, at a pinch . . . Is she discreet, your pretty Madame Lambrook?'

'Oh, yes!'

'I'll give you the key. Don't break my little knick-knacks. I'm attached to them. The electric kettle, for the tea, is in a little green cupboard to the left as you go in. You can't possibly lose your way about; I've just got one room to work (!) in, another to talk in, and a bathroom. You'll find the biscuits, the Château-Yquem, the arrack and the ginger brandy in the same cupboard. Next Thursday?'

'Next Thursday. Thank you, Marcel.'

He is a little blackguard, but at this moment I could positively hug him. When he had gone, a wild joy sent me pacing from one window to the other, with my hands behind my back and whistling my loudest.

He has *given* me the key!

The tiny key of a Fichet lock made a lump in my purse; I could feel it against my palm. I was taking Rézi there, in the crazy hope that we were hastening towards a 'solution'. To see her in secret, to keep my dear Renaud right out of this business which doesn't concern him . . . I love him too much – oh, indeed I do – to be able to see him mixed up in these intrigues without feeling appallingly uncomfortable . . .

Rézi accompanied me meekly, amused at the idea, happy that my severity had melted at last after a week of sulking.

It was warm. In the victoria, she opened the boyish jacket of her rough blue serge suit, and sighed, turning her head to get some air. Secretly, I studied the simple, fleeting line of her profile; the small girl's nose, the lashes shot through with light, the velvet of the ash-blonde eyebrows . . . She held my hand, waiting patiently, and now and then leant forward a little to look at a flower-barrow that puffed its damp fragrance at us, a shop-window, or a well-dressed woman going past us. Heavens, how sweet she was! Wouldn't anyone say she loved me, that she wanted no one but me?

We arrived at the address in the Chausée d'Antin. A big

courtyard, then a little door, a minute, well-kept staircase and landings so small that you practically had to stand on one foot. Having climbed three flights without pausing, I stopped: the air already smelt of Marcel, sandalwood and new-mown hay, with the faintest whiff of ether. I opened the door.

'Wait, Rézi, we can only go through one at a time!'

Honestly, I wasn't exaggerating! This doll's flat amused me immensely at first sight. An embryonic hall led to a scrap of a study; only the bedroom-drawing-room attained normal proportions.

Like two cats in a strange house, we advanced step by step, stopping to examine every piece of furniture, every picture-frame . . . Too many scents, too many scents . . .

'Look, Claudine, there's an aquarium on the mantelpiece.'

'See – fishes with three tails . . .'

'Oh! There's one with fins that look exactly like flounces! What's this, an incense-burner?'

'No, an ink-pot, I imagine . . . Or a coffee-cup . . . or something else.'

'What marvellous old material, darling! It would make heavenly revers on the jacket of a suit . . . Look at that charming little goddess with her arms crossed.'

'It's a little god.'

'No, Claudine, you're wrong!'

'One can't see properly; there's a drapery. Ow! Don't sit down where I did, Rézi – on the arms of this green English chair!'

'Goodness, you're right! What a fantastic notion, these sort of shiny wooden lance-heads! You could impale yourself on them! Oh, quick, do come and look, my little shepherd!'

I didn't like her calling me 'my little shepherd'; it is one of my Renaud's special names for me. I felt offended with her, but even more with him.

'Look at what?'

'His portrait!'

I joined her in the drawing-room-bedroom. It was unmistakably a portrait of Marcel dressed as a Byzantine lady. A rather curious pastel, boldly coloured, but feebly drawn. Red hair, coiled in plaits over the ears, the forehead loaded with jewels, she . . . he . . . oh, I give up! Marcel was holding one loose panel of the stiff, transparent dress away from him, with an affected gesture. The dress itself was of gauze, heavily embroidered with pearls, dripping down straight, like a curtain of rain. Between the folds you could see the pink of the tapering hips, the calf and the slender knee. With his face looking thinner, and his disdainful eyes bluer under the red hair, it was quite definitely Marcel.

Gazing at it dreamingly, with Rézi leaning against my shoulder, another picture came back into my mind. I visualized again the dark, ambiguous youth of Bronzino's brilliant portrait in the Louvre who had so suddenly vanquished me . . .

'What pretty arms that boy has!' sighed Rézi. 'Pity he's got queer tastes . . .'

'Pity for whom?' I asked, my suspicions promptly roused.

'For his family, of course.'

She laughed and put up her laughing mouth for a kiss. My mind switched to other things.

'Oh, yes . . . What concerns me now is where does he sleep?'

'He doesn't lie down . . . he sits up. Going to bed is far too ordinary.'

In spite of what she said, I had found a kind of narrow bed-recess behind a pink velvet curtain. In it was a divan draped in the same pink velvet, patterned with greyish-green plane leaves like the imprints of five fingers. I pressed an electric push-button and amused myself by flooding this altar with the light that poured down from an inverted crystal flower . . . It *would* be an orchid!

Rézi pointed a slim forefinger at the cushions strewn on the divan:

'There's all you need to prove that no woman's ever laid her head here . . .'

I laughed at her malicious perspicacity. The well-chosen cushions were all covered in rough brocade or embroidered with spangles or gold and silver thread. A woman's hair would have got pitifully tangled by them.

'All right, we'll remove them, Rézi.'

'Let's remove them, Claudine . . .'

126

Perhaps that afternoon will be our most charming memory. I was unrestrained, and less harsh. She displayed her usual ardour, her usual submission to being mastered, and the inverted flower shed its opalescent light over our brief repose . . .

A little while afterwards, from down below, came the sound of a tinny, broken-down piano and an equally broken-down tenor combining to hammer out insistently:

Jadis – vivait – en Nor-mandie . . .

At first it was annoying to have such an acute sense of rhythm as I have. But I got used to it. I adapted myself to it. And then it wasn't annoying any more . . . on the contrary.

Jadis – vivait en Nor . . .

If anyone had ever foretold to me that, one day, a tune in six-eight time from *Robert le Diable* would affect me to the point of bringing a lump into my throat . . . But it needed a very special concatenation of circumstances.

About six o'clock, when Rézi, appeased, was asleep with her arms round my neck, the doorbell rang so imperiously that it shattered our nerves. Terrified, she stifled a scream and dug all her nails into the back of my neck. Reared up on one elbow, I listened.

'Darling, don't be frightened. There's nothing to be afraid of. Someone's made a mistake . . . One of Marcel's friends – he can't have warned them all that he wouldn't be here.'

Reassured, she uncovered her white face and lay back, in a disarray that could not have been more like a 'gay' eighteenth-century print. But, once again, came that *trrr* . . .

She leapt up and began to get dressed. Terrified as she was, her conjurer's fingers did not falter. The ringing went on, insistent, persistent; it was intelligent and teasing, it played tunes on the bell. I clenched my teeth with nervous irritation.

My poor friend, pale and already ready to leave, clasped her hands over her ears. The corners of her mouth quivered each time the ringing started up again. I took pity on her.

'Now, now, Rézi. It's obviously a friend of Marcel's.'

'A friend of Marcel's! Goodness, can't you hear the malice, the purposefulness of those exasperating rings? . . . Nonsense. It's someone who knows we're here. If my husband . . .'

'Oh! You've no courage!'

'Thanks! It's easy to be brave with a husband like yours!'

I said no more. What was the good? I hooked up my corset-belt. As soon as I was dressed, I tiptoed to the door, silent as a cat, and strained my ears. I could hear nothing but that ringing, that infernal ringing!

At last, after a final, prolonged trill, a kind of exclamation mark, I heard light footsteps running away . . .

'Rézi! He's gone!'

'At last! Don't let's leave at once; someone may be spying on us . . . If you think I'll ever come back here! . . .'

What a sad ending to that meeting that was to have no sequel! My pretty coward was in such a hurry to leave me, to get right away from this building and this neighbourhood, that I dared not ask to go back with her . . . She went downstairs ahead of me, while I stayed behind to switch off the inverted flower and pick up the spangled cushions. Marcel's portrait stared at me with its contemptuous chin and its painted, tight-shut lips.

Today I was confronted with the original of the compromising Byzantine pastel, now wearing a tight, very short black jacket. He was sizzling with curiosity, just as in the days when he was so violently intrigued by Luce.

'Well, how about yesterday?'

'Really, I must thank you. What a delicious little temple you have there! It's worthy of you.'

He bowed.

'Of you too.'

'Too kind. I found your portrait particularly interesting. I'm delighted to know that your soul is a contemporary of Constantine's.'

'It's the rage nowadays . . . Tell me, are you neither of you greedy? Didn't even my Château-Yquem – it's a present from Grandmother – tempt you?'

'No. Curiosity muzzled all our other instincts.'

'Oh! *curiosity*,' he said sceptically, with the smile in his portrait . . . 'What good little housewives you are . . . I found everything in perfect order. I hope, at least, you weren't disturbed?'

His flashing smile, that look so swiftly darted, then withdrawn . . . Oh, the little beast, it was he who had rung – or got someone to ring . . . I ought to have suspected that! But I wasn't going to let that wicked boy catch me out.

'No, not in the slightest. The calm of a well-ordered house. I believe someone did ring once . . . but, again, I couldn't be sure. At that moment I was completely absorbed in contemplating . . . your little androgynous goddess, the one with the folded arms . . .'

That would teach him! And, as we are both good deceivers, he assumed the expression of a satisfied host.

TWELVE

A LETTER FROM Montigny that I was obliged to read aloud in order to understand it, the writing was so hieroglyphic.

'Aren't you going to come and see us, my little maidie? The big "imp's-thigh" rose-bush wants to flower; it's nearly out. And the little "weepy ash" has grown a lot. Monsieur is as usual.'

Monsieur was 'as usual' – I didn't doubt that, Mélie! The weeping ash had grown, good. And the big 'nymph's-thigh' rose-bush was going to flower. It's so lovely, it covers an entire wall, it flowers hurriedly, abundantly, tirelessly, and exhausts itself towards the autumn, after constant reflowerings and fresh bursts of fragrant life; it's like a thoroughbred horse that will work itself to death . . . 'The nymph's-thigh rose tree wants to flower.' At this news, I felt the fibre that binds me to Montigny revive, full of new sap. It wants to flower! . . . I thrilled with a little of the proud joy of a mother who has been told: 'Your son is going to get all the prizes!'

All my vegetable family was calling me. My forebear, the old walnut-tree, was growing old waiting for me. Under the clematis, it would soon be raining stars . . .

But I can't, I can't. What would Rézi do if I were away? I don't want to leave Renaud in her vicinity; my poor giant is such a lover of women and she is so . . . lovable!

Take Renaud with me? Rézi all alone, Rézi in the dry, scorching Paris of summertime, alone with her desires and her tastes for intrigue . . . She would deceive me.

Heavens! Is it true that four months have gone by in just drifting from hour to hour, alternating between kisses and sulks? I have done nothing during all this time, nothing at all but wait. When I leave her, I wait for the day when I shall see her again; when I am with her, I wait for her pleasure, swift or slow in coming, to yield me a lovelier, sincerer Rézi. When Renaud is with us, I wait for him to go and wait for Rézi's departure so that I may talk to my Renaud a little while, without jealousy or bitterness, because, since Rézi, he seems to love me more than ever.

This would go and happen! I have fallen ill, and now three whole weeks have been wasted. Influenza, a chill, overstrain – the doctor who is attending me can call it what he likes. I've had a very high temperature and a great deal of pain in my head. But, fundamentally, I'm robust.

Dear big Renaud, how much I appreciated your gentleness. Never have I known you take so much pains to talk in a moderate, cadenced, rounded tone of voice . . .

Rézi has looked after me too, in spite of the fear of appearing ugly to her that made me hide my burning face in my arms. Sometimes her way of looking at Renaud and her way of sitting on the edge of my bed 'for his benefit', with one knee raised, as if she were gracefully riding side-saddle, in a chip hat and a *broderie anglaise* dress with a velvet belt shocked me. Her whole way of going on was too affected and coquettish for someone visiting a sick friend. Thanks to my temperature I was able to scream 'Go away!' to her and she really believed I was delirious. I also thought that whenever she entered, I saw Renaud smile as if a puff of cool wind had blown in . . .

I felt resentful of my friend's fresh beauty and her unshadowed, matt ivory cheeks. And though, when she left, she very gently laid long-stemmed, black-red roses on the couch where I was recovering my strength, the moment she had gone, I snatched up the hand-glass hidden under the cushions and stared for a long time at my bleached pallor, thinking of her with jealous rancour . . .

'Renaud, is it true the trees on the boulevards are already turning rusty?'

'Yes, it's true, little girl. Would you like to come to Montigny? You'd see greener ones there.'

'They're too green . . . Renaud, I could go out today. I'm feeling so well. I ate all the lean part of a cutlet after my egg, I drank a glass of Asti and picked at some grapes . . . Are you going out?'

Standing in front of the window of his 'work sanctum', he looked at me undecidedly.

'I'd simply love to go out with a handsome husband like you. That grey suit is very becoming, that piqué waistcoat accentuates your distinguished Second Empire look I like so much . . . Is it for me that you're so young today?'

He reddened a little under his dark skin and smoothed his long, silver moustache.

'You know quite well it hurts me when you talk about my age . . .'

'Who's talking about your age? On the contrary, I'm seriously afraid that your youth is going to last as long as you do, like a disease you're born with. Take me out with you, Renaud! I feel strong enough to stagger the whole world!'

My grandiloquence did not make him decide in my favour.

'Certainly not, my Claudine. The doctor told you: "Not before Sunday." Today's Friday. Just another forty-eight hours' patience, my darling bird. Ah! Here comes a friend who'll know how to keep you at home . . .'

He profited by Rézi's entrance to make a hasty exit. This was entirely unlike the Renaud I knew, who was so anxious to please me, however contrary to the dictates of prudence . . . That doctor was a fool!

'Why are you making such a face, Claudine?'

She was so pretty that I relaxed my frown. Blue, blue, blue, in a blue at once misty and frothy as soap-suds.

'Rézi, the fairies have washed their linen in the water of your dress.'

She smiled, sitting close against my hip. I was looking at her from below. A long dimple, like an exclamation mark, divided her obstinate chin. Her nostrils described the simple, classic curve I used to admire in Fanchette's little nose. I sighed.

'Oh dear, I wanted to go out, and that idiot of a doctor doesn't want me to. But, at least, *you'll* stay with me, won't you? Do! Give me your freshness, the breeze that ripples in your skirt, and flutters the wings of your leafy hat . . . Do stay with me, tell me about the streets and the sun-baked trees . . . and about what little affection you have left for me since our separation.'

But she refused to sit down, and, all the time she was talking to me, her eyes kept darting from one window to another, as if she were looking for a way of escape.

'Oh! I'm too miserable for words! My sweet, I'd have liked to spend the day with you, especially as you're all alone . . . It's such a long time, Claudine darling, since your mouth was close to mine!'

She bent down caressingly, offering me her moist, shining teeth, but I turned away.

'No. I must smell of fever. Off you go and have your nice walk.'

'Don't think I'm walking for pleasure, Claudine darling! It's a dreary duty expedition. Tomorrow's the anniversary of my engagement – there's nothing to laugh about! – and I'm in the habit of giving my husband a present that day.'

'Well?'

'Well, this year I've gone and forgotten my duty as a grateful spouse. And I must rush off, so that Mr Lambrook shall find something or other under his mitred table-napkin tonight – a cigar-case, some pearl studs, a case of dynamite – well, anyway, *something*! Otherwise it means three weeks of icy silence, oh, no reproaches – that would offend his dignity . . . Lord!' she cried, raising her clenched fists. 'And there's the Transvaal needing men! What the hell is he doing here?'

Her voluble, self-conscious bantering filled me with extreme mistrust.

'But, Rézi, why don't you entrust your purchase to the infallible taste of a manservant?'

'I did think of that. But all the domestics, except my "Abigail", are under my husband's thumb.'

Decidedly, she had set her heart on going out.

133

'Run along, virtuous spouse, go and celebrate the feast of Saint Lambrook.'

She had already pulled down her white veil.

'If I'm back before six, could you put up with a little more of me?'

How pretty she was bending forward like that! Her skirt, swirled tight round her by the swiftness of her movement, revealed all the lines of her body . . . I was moved only to a Platonic admiration. Was my convalescence to blame? I no longer felt the old desire beating up on great, tempestuous wings . . . And, besides, she had refused to sacrifice Saint Lambrook's Day for me!

'It all depends. Come up, anyway, and you'll be rewarded according to your merits . . . *No*, I tell you, I smell of fever!'

So, there I was, all alone. I yawned, I read three pages, I walked about the room. I began a letter to Papa, then I became absorbed in assiduously polishing my nails. Seated at the dressing-table, I cast a glance every now and then at the mirror like someone watching the clock. I didn't look so awful, after all . . . My curls were a little longer; that was not unattractive. That white collar, that little red muslin blouse with hundreds of fine white stripes, irresistibly suggested a walk in the street . . . I read in the glass what my eyes had decided. It was soon done! A black-banded boater, a jacket over my arm so that Renaud couldn't scold me for taking risks, and I was out of doors.

Heavens, how hot it was! It didn't surprise me that the nymph's-thigh rose-bush was flowering with zest. Filthy place, this Paris! I felt light; I had grown thinner. The fresh air was a little intoxicating, but I got used to it as I walked. I had no more thoughts in my head than a dog being taken out after being cooped up in a flat for a week of rainy days.

Without doing so on purpose, I mechanically took the route to the rue Goethe . . . I smiled when I arrived outside number 59 and I threw a friendly glance up at the white net curtains that veiled the windows of the second floor . . .

Ah! the curtain had stirred! . . . That tiny movement riveted me to the pavement, stiff as a doll. Whoever was up in 'our' flat? Maybe it was the wind blowing in from a

134

window on the courtyard that had lifted that net . . . But while my logical self was reasoning, the beast in me, bitten by a suspicion, then suddenly enraged, had guessed before it had understood.

I raced across the street; I climbed the two flights, as in a nightmare, treading on steps of cotton-wool that sank and rebounded under my feet. I was going to drag with all my might on the brass bell-pull, ring till I brought the house down . . . No. *They* would not come!

I waited a minute, my hand on my heart. That wretched banal gesture cruelly brought back a phrase of Claire's, the girl who made her First Communion with me: 'Life's just like it is in books, isn't it?'

I pulled the brass handle timidly, starting at the unfamiliar sound of that bell that had never rung for us . . . And for two long seconds, seized with a childish cowardice, I kept saying to myself: 'Oh! If only they wouldn't open it!'

The approaching step brought all my courage back on a wave of anger. Renaud's voice inquired irritably:

'Who's there?'

I had no breath left. I leant against the sham marble wall that chilled my arm. And the sound of the door he had opened a little way made me want to die . . .

. . . but not for long. I *had* to pull myself together! Hell, I was Claudine! I was Claudine! I flung off my fear like a coat. I said: 'Open the door, Renaud, or I'll scream.' I looked straight into the face of the man who opened it; he was completely dressed. He recoiled, in sheer astonishment. And he let out one mild expletive; like a gambler annoyed by ill luck:

'The deuce!'

The impression of being the stronger stiffened my courage still more. I was Claudine! And I said:

'I saw someone at the window from down below. So I came up to say "Hullo" to you.'

'It was wicked of me to do it,' he muttered.

He made no move to try to stop me, but stood back to let me pass, then followed me.

In a flash, I crossed the little drawing-room and raised the

135

flowered curtain in the doorway . . . Ah! Just as I thought! Rézi was there, of course she was there – and putting on her clothes again . . . In corset and knickers, her lace and linen petticoat over her arm, her hat on her head, just as for me . . . I shall always see that fair-skinned face decomposing, looking as if it were dying under my gaze. I almost envied her for being so frightened. She stared at my hands and I saw her thin lips go white and dry. Without taking her eyes off me, she stretched out a groping arm towards her dress. I took one step forward. She nearly fell, and threw up her arms to protect her face. That gesture, which revealed her downy armpits whose warmth I so often inhaled, unleashed a hurricane in me. I would snatch up that water-jug and hurl it . . . or maybe that chair. The lines of the furniture quivered before my eyes like hot air over the fields . . .

Renaud, who had followed me, lightly touched my shoulder. He was hesitant, a trifle pale, but, above all, worried. I asked him, speaking with difficulty:

'What are you . . . you two . . . doing here?'

He smiled nervously, in spite of himself.

'Why . . . we were waiting for you, as you see.'

I was dreaming . . . or he had gone out of his mind . . . I turned again towards the woman there. While my eyes were averted from her, she had put on the blue dress in which the fairies had washed their linen . . . *She* would not have dared to smile!

'Life's just like it is in books, isn't it?' No, sweet Claire. In books the woman who arrives on the scene fires two shots at least to avenge herself. Or else she goes off, slamming the door on the guilty couple after crushing them with one contemptuous remark . . . But *I* could find no gesture; the truth was I had not the faintest idea what I ought to do. You don't learn the part of an outraged wife in five minutes, just like that.

I was still barring the door. I thought Rézi was going to faint. How odd that would be! *He*, at least, wasn't frightened. Like me, he was following, with more interest than emotion, the succeeding phases of terror on Rézi's face. He seemed finally to have grasped that this hour was not going to bring the three of us together.

136

'Listen, Claudine . . . I meant to tell you . . .'

With a sweep of my arm, I cut short his sentence. In any case, he seemed none too anxious to continue it, and he shrugged his left shoulder with a rather fatalistic air of resignation.

It was Rézi who roused all my fury! I advanced on her slowly. I could see myself advancing on her. This double consciousness made me uncertain what I meant to do. Was I going to strike her, or only increase her shameful fear to swooning-point?

She drew back and moved round behind the little table on which the tea stood. She had reached the wall! She was going to escape me! Ah! I wasn't going to let her.

But already her hand was on the door-curtain, she was groping at it, walking backwards, keeping her eyes fixed on me. Involuntarily, I stooped down to pick up a stone . . . There were no stones . . . She had disappeared.

I let my arms drop; all my energy suddenly drained away.

Then we were, the two of us, looking at each other. Renaud's face was – almost – his kind, everyday face. He looked troubled. His beautiful eyes were a little sad. Oh heavens, the next moment he was going to say: 'Claudine,' and if I voiced my anger, if I let the strength that still sustained me ebb away in reproaches and tears, I should leave the place on his arm, plaintive and forgiving . . . I *wouldn't*! I was . . . I was Claudine, hang it! And besides, I should be too furious with him for having made me forgive him.

I had waited too long. He stepped forward, he said: 'Claudine . . .'

I leapt back, and, instinctively, I started to flee, like Rézi. Only *I* was fleeing from myself.

I did well to make my escape. The street, the glance I threw up at the betraying curtain revived all my pride and resentment. Moreover, I knew now where I was going.

It took less than a quarter of an hour to rush home in a cab, grab my suitcase, and be downstairs again, having flung my key on a table. I had some money, not much, but enough.

'Gare de Lyon, driver.'

137

Before getting into the train, I sent a telegram to Papa, then another to Renaud: 'Send clothes and linen to Montigny for an indefinite stay.'

THIRTEEN

THOSE CORNFLOWERS ON the wall, faded from blue to grey, shadows of flowers on a paler paper . . . That chintz curtain with the fantastic pattern – yes, there was the monstrous fruit, the apple with eyes in it . . . Over and over again I had seen them in my dreams during my two years in Paris, but never so vividly . . .

This time, from the depths of my transparent sleep, I actually heard the creak of the pump!

I sat up, with a start, in my little four-poster. The first smiling welcome of the bedroom of my childhood made me burst into floods of tears. Tears as bright as the sunbeam that danced in golden coins on the windowpanes, as soothing to my eyes as the flowers on the grey wallpaper. So it was really true that I was here, in this bedroom! There was no other thought in my head till I came to wipe my eyes with a little pink handkerchief that had no connection with Montigny . . .

My unhappiness dried my tears. I had been hurt. A salutary hurt? I could almost believe it was, for, after all, I could not be thoroughly unhappy in Montigny, in this house . . . Oh! there was my little ink-stained desk! It still contained all my school exercise-books: *Arithmetic* . . . *Dictation*. For in Mademoiselle's day, we no longer put *Sums* or *Spelling*. *Dictation, Arithmetic* sounded more distinguished, more 'Secondary School' . . .

Hard nails scratched on the door and scrabbled at the keyhole. An anguished, imperious 'Meow!' summoned me to open it . . . 'O my darling girl, how beautiful you are! My ideas are in such a muddle that, for a moment, I'd forgotten you, Fanchette!' I took her into my arms, into my bed, and she thrust her wet nose and her cold teeth against my chin, so excited to see me again that she kneaded my bare arm with all her claws out. 'How old are you now? Five, six? I can't remember. Your white fur looks so young. You'll die young . . . like Renaud. Oh dear, that memory's gone and spoilt everything for me. Stay under my cheek so that I can forget myself, listening to all your purring machinery vibrating at full blast . . . Whatever must you have thought of me, arriving suddenly like that without any luggage? Even Papa smelt a rat!'

'Well? And where's the other animal? Your husband?' he had asked.

'He'll come as soon as he's less busy, Papa.'

I was pale and absent-minded; I was still there in the rue Goethe, between those two people who had hurt me. Though it was past ten o'clock, I refused to eat anything; all I craved for was a bed, a warm, solitary burrow where I could think and weep and hate . . . But the darkness of my old bedroom sheltered so many kindly little ghosts that they lulled me into deep, dreamless sleep.

There was a slither of slipshod feet. Mélie entered without knocking. She had dropped back at once into all the old ways. In one hand she held the little tray that had lost most of its varnish – the very same one – in the other, her left breast. She was faded and slatternly, with a touch of the procuress in her make-up, but the mere sight of her warmed my heart. What that ugly servant was bringing me in the steaming cup on the scabbed little tray was 'the philtre that annihilates the years! . . .' It smelt of chocolate, that philtre. I was dying of hunger!

'Mélie!'

'What, my precious lammy?'

'Do you love me?'

She paused long enough to put down her tray before answering, with a shrug of her flabby shoulders:

'You bet I do.'

It was true: I could feel it was true. She remained standing,

140

watching me eat. Fanchette watched me too, sitting on my feet. Both of them admire me unreservedly. Nevertheless, Mélie shook her head and weighed her left breast with a disapproving expression on her face.

'Don't look any too hearty, you don't. What have *they* been doing to you?'

'I've had influenza. I wrote and told Papa that. By the way, where *is* Papa?'

'Messing about in his den, I'll be bound. Leastways, you'll see him soon enough. Be you wanting me to fetch you a porger? I'll go get un.'

A 'porger' in our parts is a big wooden basin.

'Get un for what?' I said, slipping back into the beloved dialect.

'Why, to wash Lord Behind and Lady Titty for sure!'

'Deedy, yes. A good big one too!'

In the doorway, she turned round and asked point-blank:

'When be *he* coming . . . Monsieur Renaud?'

'Be *I* like to know? He'll write and tell you. Now, trot along, do!'

While waiting for the porger, I leant out of the window. There was nothing to be seen in the street but a tumble of roofs. On account of the very steep slope, each house has its first floor on the level of the ground floor of the one above it. I was quite certain that the slope had grown steeper in my absence! I could see the corner of the rue des Soeurs, which runs straight – I mean, crooked – to the School . . . Should I go and see Mademoiselle? No; I wasn't looking pretty enough . . . Besides, I might find little Hélène there – that future Rézi . . . No, no, no more girls, no more women! Spreading out my fingers, I shook my hand with slightly disgusted irritation, as if a long, smooth hair had got caught in my nails . . .

I slipped, barefooted, into the drawing-room . . . Those old armchairs, the very rents in them were like welcoming smiles! Here, everything was in its right place. Two penitential years in Paris had not eclipsed the gaiety of their round backs and their pretty Louis XVI feet, still whitened with a remnant of paint . . . That Mélie, what a dolt she was! The blue vase that, for fifteen years, I had always seen on the left of the green

141

vase, she had gone and put it on the right! Quickly, I restored everything to its proper place till I had completely recreated the setting in which I had lived nearly all my life. Nothing, in fact, was missing except my former gaiety, my cheerful solitude . . .

On the other side of the shutters, closed against the sun, lay the garden . . . No, garden, no, I would not go and look at you for another hour! The mere whisper of your foliage would move me too much, it was so long since I had eaten green leaves!

Papa probably thought I was asleep. Or else he had forgotten that I had arrived. No matter. In a little while, I would go into his lair and bring down a few maledictions on my head. Fanchette followed me step by step, terrified I might escape again. 'My swee-ee-eet! Have no fear! I tell you, my telegram said: *clothes and linen . . . for indefinite stay . . .*' Indefinite. What did that mean? I was no longer any too sure. But it certainly seemed to me that I was here for a long, long time . . . Ah! how good it was to give one's misery a change of scene!

My brief morning drifted by in the enchanted garden. It had grown. The temporary tenant had touched nothing, not even the grass on the paths, I believe . . .

The enormous walnut-tree bore thousands and thousands of full nuts. Just breathing in the strong, funereal smell of one of its crumpled leaves made me close my eyes. I leant against it, the protector of the garden, but its destroyer too, for the chill of its shade kills the roses. What does it matter? Nothing is lovelier than a tree – than that particular tree. At the far end, against old Madame Adolphe's wall, the twin fir-trees nodded an unsmiling greeting, stiff in their sombre raiment that serves for every season . . .

The wistaria that climbs up to the roof had lost all its charming flowers . . . So much the better! I found it hard to forgive wistaria blossom for having adorned Rézi's hair . . .

Inert at the foot of the walnut-tree, I felt myself becoming a plant again. Over there, Quail Mountain looked blue and far away; it would be fine tomorrow, if Moustiers was not covered with cloud.

'My lammykin! Look – see, a letter!'

. . . A letter . . . Already! How brief the respite had been!
Couldn't he have left me a little time, a little more of sunshine
and animal life? I felt very small and frightened, faced with the
pain about to assault me . . . Oh, to wipe out everything that
had been, wipe it out and start again quite fresh! . . .

My darling child . . .

He might just as well have stopped there. I knew everything
he was going to say. Yes, I was his child! Why had he deceived
me?

*My darling child, I cannot console myself for the pain I
have caused you. You have done what you had every right to
do and I am nothing but a wretched man who loves you and
is desolate. You know, Claudine, you must surely know that
nothing but imbecile curiosity impelled me to that, also that it
isn't about that I feel guilty: I tell you this at the risk of
making you feel even harsher towards me. But I have hurt you
and I can't get a moment's peace. I'm sending you everything
you asked for. I entrust you to the country you love.
Remember that, in spite of everything, you are my one and
only love, my one and only source of life. My 'youth' as you
used to call it when you still used to look up into my eyes and
laugh – that dismal youth of a man already old – has vanished
at one stroke with you . . .*

How it hurt, how it hurt! I sobbed, sitting there on the
ground with my head against the rough flank of the walnut-
tree. My own pain tormented me; so, alas, did his . . . I had
never before known what a 'broken heart' was, and now I
was enduring the anguish of two, and suffering even more for
his than mine . . . Renaud, Renaud! . . .

Sitting there, I gradually became numb; my sorrow slowly
congealed. My burning eyes followed the flight of a wasp, the
'frrt' of a bird, the complicated journey of a ground-beetle . . .
How blue the blue of those aconites was! a fine full-bodied
colour, strong and plebeian . . . Where did that honeyed
breath come from, smelling of attar of roses and spiced cake?
. . . It was the great nymph's-thigh rose-bush wafting me its
incense . . . That bush brought me to my feet, that were
swarming all over with ants, to go over and greet it.

143

So many roses, so many roses! I wanted to say to it: 'Rest. You have flowered enough, worked enough, exhausted enough of your strength and your fragrance . . .' It wouldn't have listened to me. It wanted to beat the rose record in number and in scent. It had stamina, it had speed, it gave everything it had. Its innumerable daughters were pretty little roses, like the ones on Holy Pictures, barely tinted at the edges of the petals, with little hearts of vivid carmine. Taken singly, they might seem slightly insipid, but who would dream of criticizing the mantle, murmurous with bees, they had thrown over this wall?

'Swine of a donkey! Will someone flay the skin of that infamous beast vomited up by the jaws of hell? . . .'

No possible doubt that was Papa giving signs of life. Delighted at the thought of seeing him, of distracting myself with his extravagant absurdity, I ran. I saw him leaning out of a window on the first floor, the library one. His beard had whitened a little, but it still poured in a tricoloured flood over his vast chest. His nostrils snorted fire and his gesture struck consternation into the universe.

'What's the matter, Papa?'

'That filthy cat has walked all over my beautiful wash-drawing with her dirty paws, ruined it for ever! She bloody well deserves to be chucked out of the window!'

So he was perpetrating wash-drawings now? I trembled a little for my darling Fanchette.

'Oh, Papa, you haven't hurt her?'

'No, of course not! But I might have done and I ought to have done, d'you hear, you daughter of a wheezy horse?'

I breathed again. Seeing him so rarely now, I had forgotten how harmless his thunderbolts were.

'And you, my Dine, are you well?'

His infinitely tender voice, that pet name of my very earliest childhood, reopened fountains of youth in me; I listened to bright, fleeting memories plashing drop by drop. Thank goodness, he had started thundering again!

'Well, she-ass, I'm talking to you, I believe?'

'Yes, Papa dear, I'm well. Are you working?'

'It's insulting to me even to doubt it. Here, read this; it

144

appeared last week; it produced an earthquake. All my oafs of colleagues pulled long faces . . .'

He threw me down the number of *Reports* that included his precious contribution.

Malacology, malacology! To thy faithful devotees thou dispensest happiness and oblivion of humanity and all its woes . . . Flicking through the little magazine (its cover was a cheerful pink), I came across the authentic slug in this word that trailed its slimy length of fifty-four letters right across the page. *Tetramethylmonophenilsulfotriparaamidotriphenylmethane* . . . Alas! I could hear Renaud's laugh at the discovery of such a gem.

'Would you let me keep this, Papa? Or is it your only copy?'

'No,' he replied from his window, like Jupiter from Olympus. 'I've ordered ten thousand private reprints of it from Gauthier-Villars.'

'That was wise. What time do we have lunch?'

'Ask the domestic staff. I am nothing but a brain. I don't eat. I think!'

With a noise like thunder, he slammed his window shut and the sunlight glittered on the panes.

I knew him; this man who was nothing but a brain would shortly be 'thinking' a large beef steak.

My entire day drifted by in searching step by step, crumb by crumb, for all the fragments of my childhood scattered in the corners of the old house; in staring, through the bars of the gate that the powerful wistaria had wrenched out of shape, at Quail Mountain changing and growing paler, then turning purple in the distance. The thick woods whose rich, dense green took on a blue tinge towards evening, those I would leave till tomorrow. I was not ready to love them yet . . . Today, I dressed my wound, and nursed my hurt in a sheltered place. Too much light, too much clean wind and the green briars blossoming with wild roses might rip off the light cotton-wool of healing that swathed my sorrow.

In the reddening evening, I listened to the kindly garden settling down to sleep. Above my head, the black shape of a little bat zigzagged in silent flight . . . A Saint-Jean pear-tree, lavish and hurried, dropped its round fruits one by one – those pears that are sleepy as soon as they are ripe and bring tenacious wasps down with them as they fall . . . Five, six, ten wasps in the hole of one little pear . . . They go on eating as they fall, merely beating the air with their light wings . . . That was just how Rézi's golden lashes used to flutter under my lips.

This reminder of my treacherous mistress did not make me double up inwardly with the pain I dreaded. Ah, I had been right in my surprise that I had not loved *her*.

Whereas there was something else I could not conjure up without a torturing pang, without clasping my hands in anguish – Renaud's tall figure in the dimness of that flowered bedroom, watching my face for my decision, his sad eyes fearing the irrevocable . . .

'My pettikins, a telegram for you!'

Honestly, it was too much! I turned round, menacing and furious, ready to tear the paper to shreds.

'It's reply paid.'

I read: *Urgently request news of health.*

. . . He had not dared say more. He had been conscious of Papa, of Mélie, of Mademoiselle Mathieu, the post-mistress.

I was conscious of them too, in my reply: *Comfortable journey. Father very well.*

I cried in my sleep but I cannot remember what I dreamt. Yet it was a dream Day was just breaking; it was only three o'clock. The hens were still asleep, only the sparrows were twittering, making a noise like gravel being shifted. It was going to be fine; the dawn was blue . . .

I wanted, as I used to do as a little girl, to get up before the sun and go to the wood of Fredonnes to catch the nocturnal taste of the cold spring and the last shreds of the night that retreats into the undergrowth before the first rays and buries itself there . . .

I jumped out of bed. Fanchette, asleep and deprived of the hollow between my knees, coiled herself round like a snail without so much as opening an eye. She gave a little moan, then pressed her white paw more firmly over her closed eyes. She is not interested in dewy dawns. She only cares for clear, bright nights when, sitting upright and austere as an Egyptian

146

cat-goddess, she stares interminably at the white moon moving across the sky.

My hasty dressing and that uncertain early half-light took me back to winter mornings when I used to get up shivering and set off to school, through the cold and the unswept snow. A skimpy little urchin, brave under my red hood, I would crack boiled chestnuts with my teeth as I slid along on my small pointed *sabots*.

I passed through the garden and climbed over the spikes of the gate. I wrote on the kitchen floor, with a piece of charcoal: 'Claudine has gone out. She'll be back for lunch.' Before climbing over the gate, with my skirt hitched up, I smiled at *my* house, for nothing is more my very own than that big granite dwelling with its peeling shutters open day and night over unsuspicious windows. The mauve slate of the roof was adorned with close-shaven little yellow lichens and, on the flag of the weathercock, two swallows were puffing out their white chests, offering them to be scratched by the first sharp rays of sunlight.

My unwonted appearance in the street disturbed dogs who were doing duty as scavengers, and grey cats fled silently, their backs arched. Safe on a window-sill, they gazed after me with yellow eyes . . . In a minute or two, they would come down again, when the noise of my footsteps had decreased round the turning . . .

These Paris boots were no good at all for Montigny. I would get some other, less elegant ones, with little nails in the soles . . .

The exquisite cold of the blue dusk struck my skin, so long unused to it, and pinched my ears. But up there on the heights, lilac mists drifted like gauzy sails and the edges of the roofs had suddenly turned a violent orange-pink . . . I almost ran towards the light till I reached the Saint-Jean gate, half-way up the hill, where a cheerful tumble-down house, stuck there all by itself at the edge of the town, guards the entrance to the fields. There I stopped, heaving a great sigh . . .

Had I reached the end of my troubles? Up here, would I feel the last impact of the cruel blow die away? In that valley, narrow as a candle, I had laid all the dreams of sixteen years of solitary childhood . . . I seemed to see them sleeping there still, veiled in a milky mist that rippled and flowed like a sea . . .

The clatter of a shutter being thrown open chased me away from the heap of stones where I had been day-dreaming in the wind that almost froze my lips . . . It was not the people of Montigny I had come out to see. What I wanted was to descend the hill, go through that bed of mist, climb the sandy yellow path on the other side up to the woods whose crests were tipped with fiery rose . . . Onwards!

I walked on and on, in anxious haste, keeping my eyes on the ground all along the hedgerows, as if I were searching for the herb that would heal me . . .

I returned home half an hour after midday, more exhausted and dishevelled than if three poachers had set upon me in the woods. But while Mélie moaned and lamented, I stared at my reflection with a passive smile. My tired face was striped with a pink scratch near my lip, my hair was matted with burrs, my soaking skirt was embroidered with little, green hairy beads of wild millet. My blue linen skirt was split under the arms, and a warm, damp smell rose up in my nostrils, that smell that so madly excited Ren . . . No, I never wanted to think of him again!

How beautiful the woods were! How soft the light! How cold the dew on the edges of the grassy ditches! I had been too late to find that charming population of small, frail flowers in the fields and copses, forget-me-not and bladder campion, daffodils and spring daisies; Solomon's seal and lily of the valley had long since shed their hanging bells. But at least I had been able to bathe my bare hands and trembling legs in thick, deep grass, sprawl my tired limbs on the dry velvet of moss and pine-needles, rest without a thought in my head, baked by the fierce, mounting sun . . . I was penetrated with sunlight, rustling with breezes, echoing with crickets and birdsong, like a room open on a garden . . .

'That's a nice sight, to be sure! A pretty dress like that!' scolded Mélie.

'Don't care. I've got other ones. Oh, Mélie, I don't think I'd have come home if I didn't need my lunch so! . . . But I'm simply dying of hunger.'

'That's a good thing. The food's all cooked . . . But I ask, where's your sense got to, doing such a thing? And Monsieur yelling after you everywhere and rolling his eyes like a stuck pig. You're just the same as ever. You little tramp, you!'

I had run about so much and looked at so much and loved so much that morning that I stayed in the garden all the afternoon. The kitchen garden, that I had not visited yet, presented me with warm apricots and peaches, which I ate afterwards, lying on my stomach under the big fir-trees with an old Balzac between my elbows.

How marvellously light-hearted I felt, how blissfully tired from physical exertion! Didn't that mean I was happy again, that I had forgotten everything and recovered my joyous solitude of the old days?

I might have deceived myself into believing it, but no, Mélie was wrong; I wasn't 'the same as ever'. As the day declined, the wound began to throb again, the uneasiness returned, the torturing uneasiness that forced me to keep moving, to keep changing from one room, one chair, one book to another as one tries to find a cool place in a fever-tossed bed . . . I went into the kitchen and, after long hesitation – I was helping Mélie beat a mayonnaise that refused to thicken – I finally asked her, in a casual voice:

'There weren't any letters for me today, were there?'

'No, my lammy; nothing came but Monsieur's papers.'

I went to sleep so tired that my ears buzzed and the exhausted muscles of my calves went on quivering automatically. But my slumber was not pleasant; it was shot through with confused dreams, dominated by a nerve-racking sensation of waiting for something. It was so strong that I lingered on in bed this morning, between Fanchette and my cooling chocolate.

Fanchette, convinced that I have come back solely for her sake, has enjoyed perfect bliss since my return. A little too perfect, perhaps. I don't torment her enough. She misses my constant teasing of the old days when I used to hold her upright on her hind-paws, or dangle her by her tail, or swing her to and fro, two paws gripped in either hand, crying:

149

'Here's a fine white hare, weighing eight pounds!' Now I am always gentle. I caress her without pinching her or biting her ears . . . Really, Fanchette, one can't have everything; look at me, for example . . .

Who was that walking up the front doorstep? The postman, surely . . . As long as Renaud hadn't written to me!

Mélie would have brought me his letter by now . . . She wasn't coming . . . All the same, I listened with my ears and my nostrils stretched to their utmost . . . She wasn't coming . . . He hadn't written . . . So much the better! Let him forget and allow me to forget!

That sigh, what did it mean? It was a sigh of relief. What else *could* it be? But if Claudine was reassured, why was she trembling all over? . . . Why hadn't he written? Because I hadn't answered him . . . Because he was frightened of making me even angrier . . . Or else he had written, and torn up his letter . . . He had missed the post . . . He was ill!

With one bound, I was out of bed, pushing away the dishevelled cat, who blinked at this rude awakening. This movement restored me to consciousness; I felt thoroughly ashamed of myself . . .

Mélie was such a dawdler . . . She would have put the letter down on a corner of the kitchen table, beside the butter they bring wrapped in two beet leaves . . . That butter would make a greasy mark on the letter. I pulled a cord that let loose a din like a convent bell.

'Is it for your hot water, my pet?'

'Yes, of course . . . Oh, Mélie! Didn't the postman bring anything for me?'

'Nothing, my lamb.'

Her faded blue eyes crinkled up with ribald affection.

'Aha! Hankering after your man? You blessed little newly-wed, you! Fair itching for him.'

She went off, chuckling very low. I turned my back to my looking-glass so as not to see the expression on my face.

Having finally recaptured my courage, I climbed up, preceded by Fanchette, to the attic where I had so often taken refuge when it rained for days on end. It is huge and dim; laundered sheets hang over the wooden rollers of the drier; a pile of half-gnawed-away books occupies an entire corner; an antique night-commode, with one foot missing, gapes open, awaiting a ghostly behind. A great wicker hamper conceals remnants of wallpapers that date back to the Restoration; plum-coloured stripes on a bilious yellow ground; imitation green trellises overgrown with strange vegetation among which fluttered improbable marrow-green birds . . . All this jumbled pell-mell with the tattered remains of an old herbarium in which I used to admire the delicate skeletons of rare plants from goodness knows where before I destroyed them . . . Some of them were still left, and I turned over the pages, inhaling the old dust with its sweetish, faintly chemist's shop smell, and the odour of mildewed paper, dead plants and lime blossoms gathered last week, spread out to dry on a sheet . . . When I pushed up the skylight I saw the same old little landscape framed in its aperture when I raised my head; a distant, complete little landscape with a wood to the left, a sloping meadow, and a red roof in the corner . . . It was composed with care, naïve and charming.

From below came the sound of the door-bell. I listened to doors opening, indistinct voices, something like a heavy piece of furniture being dragged along . . . Poor, unhappy Claudine, how the slightest thing upsets you now! . . . I could not bear to stay up there any longer; I would rather go down to the kitchen.

'Wherever had you got to, my pet? I looked for you; then I thought you'd gone off tramping again . . . It's your trunk Monsieur Renaud's sent express. Racalin's took it to your bedroom by the back stairs . . .'

That big parchment trunk depressed and upset me as much as if it had been a piece of furniture from *over there* . . . One of its sides still bore a large red label with white letters: HÔTEL DES BERGUES.

It dated from our honeymoon . . . I had begged for that label to be left on because it enabled the trunk to be seen a long way away at stations . . . At the Hôtel des Bergues . . . it had rained all the time, we had never gone out . . .

I pushed up the lid violently, as if I wanted to throw off the searing, beloved memory that rose up before me, wearing the

151

face of hope.

At first sight, I did not think the maid had forgotten anything to speak of. The maid . . . I saw traces of other hands than hers here . . . It was not she who had put in, under the summer blouses and the layers of fresh, fine underlinen threaded with new ribbons, the little green leather case. Inside it, the ruby Renaud had given me shone lucent, like transparent blood, like rich, mellow wine . . . I hardly dared to touch it. No, no; let it go on sleeping in the little green case!

In the lower compartment lay my dresses, their bodices empty and their sleeves like deflated balloons; three simple dresses that I can keep here. But shall I also keep that enchanting little old silver box here, a present from him, like the ruby, like everything I possess? It had been filled with my favourite sweets, extra sugary fondants and chocolate creams . . . Renaud, wicked Renaud, if only you knew how bitter sweets taste, wetted with hot tears! . . .

I hesitated now over lifting each layer, for the past clung to every fold and everything spoke of the tender, imploring solicitude of the man who had betrayed me . . . Everything here was full of him; he had smoothed the folded underclothes with his own hands, he had tied the ribbons of those sachets they were packed in . . .

Working slowly, my eyes misty with tears, I lingered long over the emptying of this reliquary . . .

I would have liked to linger even longer! Right at the bottom, in one of my little morocco mules, a white letter was rolled up. I knew perfectly well that I should read it . . . but how cold that sealed paper felt! How unpleasantly it crackled under my trembling fingers! I had to read it, if only to silence that odious little noise . . .

'My poor, adored child, I am sending you all that remains to me of you, everything that still kept your scent lingering here, a little of your presence. My darling, you who believe in the soul of things, I still hope that these will speak of me without anger to you. Will you forgive me, Claudine? I am mortally lonely. Give me back – not now, later on, when you feel you can – not my wife, but just the dear little daughter you have taken away. Because my heart is bursting with grief at the thought of your pale, intense little face smiling at your father while all that remains to *me* is the cruel face of Marcel. I implore you to remember, when you are less unhappy, that one line from you would be as dear and blessed to me as a promise . . .'

'Wherever be you off to now? And lunch on the table, waiting for you!'

'It'll have to be disappointed. I'm not having any lunch. Tell Papa . . . oh, anything you like, that I'm going to walk as far as Quail Mountain . . . I shan't be home till this evening.'

As I spoke, I was feverishly stuffing things into a little basket, the crusty top of a cottage loaf, some windfall apples, a leg of chicken pinched from the dish ready for the table . . . Definitely I was *not* lunching here! To see clear into my troubled mind, I needed the sun-striped shadow and the beauty of the woods as counsellor.

In spite of the harsh sun, I did not stop once as I followed the narrow path that leads to Les Vrimes, more of a ditch than a path, hollow and sandy like a river-bed. My footsteps sent *verdelles* scurrying away, those big, emerald-green lizards who are so timid that I have never managed to capture one. Clouds of common butterflies, beige and brown like labourers, rose up in front of me. A Camberwell beauty zigzagged past, brushing the hedge as if it were an effort to raise its heavy brown velvet wings any higher . . . At long intervals, a shallow, undulating furrow made a hollow imprint in the sand; a snake had passed there, slate-coloured and shining. Perhaps the green legs of a frog, still kicking, had protruded from its flat little tortoise-like mouth . . .

Often I turned round, to watch the ivy-clad Saracen tower and the decrepit castle growing smaller. I wanted to go as far as the little gamekeeper's lodge that, maybe a hundred years ago, lost the floorboards of its single storey, its windows, its door, and even its very name . . . For here it is called 'the-little-house-where-there-are-so-many-dirty-things-written-on-the-walls'. That's the sort of place it is. And it really is a fact that it would be impossible to see more obscenities and naïve bits of gross scatology than are carved or scrawled in charcoal there. They cover the entire length and breadth of the walls so thickly that they intertwine and they are illustrated with sketches, done with chalk or a pen-knife. But I am not concerned with the little six-sided house to which rude boys and bands of sly girls make their pilgrimage on Sundays . . . What I want is the wood it used to guard and that is never sullied by young Sunday pleasure-seekers because it is too dense, too silent, and broken by damp gulleys brimming over with ferns . . .

Ravenous, with all thought put to sleep, I ate like a wood-cutter, my basket between my knees. The sheer delight of feeling a lively animal, conscious of nothing but the flavour of crisp, crunchy bread and juicy apple! The gentle landscape awakened a sensuality in me that was almost like the rapture of the hunger I was appeasing; those dark, close-knit woods smelt like the apple, this fresh bread was as gay as the pink-tiled roof that pierced them . . .

Then, lying on my back, with my arms flung out sideways, I waited for blissful torpor.

No one in the fields. What would they be doing in them? Nothing was cultivated there. The grass grew, the dead wood fell, the game walked into the snare. Little girls on holiday from school led the sheep along the slopes and everything, at this hour, was taking a siesta, like myself. A flowering briar-bush exhaled its deceptive smell of strawberries. The low branches of a stunted oak sheltered me like the porch of a house.

While I was slithering a little way to change my bed of cool grass, a crackling of crumpled paper chased away approaching sheep. Renaud's letter palpitated inside my blouse, that imploring letter . . .

'My poor, adored child' . . . 'the dear little daughter you have taken away' . . . 'Your pale intense little face . . .'

He had written, perhaps for the first time in his life, without weighing the words he wrote, without any attempt at literary style – he who, normally, was as shocked to see a word repeated only two lines later as to find an inkstain on his finger.

I carried that letter as engaged girls do, next to my heart. That and the other one of the day before yesterday were the only two love-letters I had ever received. For, during our brief engagement, Renaud had been with me every day, and, ever since, gaily, meekly, or indifferently I had always followed him wherever his roving, worldly temperament took him . . .

What good had I done him or myself, in eighteen months? I had rejoiced in his love, been saddened by his frivolity, shocked by his ways of thinking and behaving – all this without saying a word and deliberately avoiding discussions. And more than once I had felt resentful towards Renaud for my own silence.

There had been egotism in my suffering without trying to find a remedy; there had been obstinate pride in my silent reproaches. Yet what was there he would not have done for me? I could have obtained everything from his passionate tenderness; he loved me enough to guide me – if I had guided him first. And what had I asked him for? A place for assignations!

We must begin all over again. Thank God, it was not too late to make a fresh start. 'My dear giant,' I would say to him, 'I order you to dominate me! . . .' And I would say too . . . oh, so many other things . . .

It was growing late. The sun was dipping, delicate butterflies were emerging from the woods with a hesitant, already nocturnal flight; a shy, sociable little owl appeared too early on the fringe of the wood, blinking its dazzled eyes; as the daylight faded, the undergrowth was coming alive with a thousand uneasy rustlings and little cries. But for all these things I had only inattentive ears and absently tender eyes . . . Suddenly, I was on my feet, stretching my numbed arms and cramped calves; the next moment I was rushing away towards Montigny, spurred on by the time – the time of the post, of course! I wanted to write, to write to Renaud.

I had made my resolution . . . Ah! how little it had cost me!

Dear Renaud, I find it difficult to write to you because this is the first time. And I feel I shall never be able to say all I want to say to you before the evening post goes.

I've got to ask your forgiveness for having gone away and to thank you for having let me go. It has taken me four days, all alone in my house with my misery, to understand

something you could have convinced me of in a few minutes
... All the same, I think these four days have not been wasted.

You have written me all your loving tenderness, dear giant,
without saying a word to me about Rézi, without telling me:
'You did with her just what I did, with so little difference ...'
Yet that would have been very reasonable, almost flawless as
a piece of logic. But you knew that it was not the same thing
... and I'm grateful to you for not having said it.

I don't want ever, ever again to make you unhappy, but you
must help me over this, Renaud. Yes, I am your child ...
something more than your child, an over-petted daughter
whom you ought sometimes to refuse what she asks for. I
wanted Rézi and you gave her to me like a sweet ... You've
got to teach me that some kinds of sweets are harmful and
that, if one eats them all, one must be on the lookout for bad
brands ... Don't, dear Renaud, be afraid of making your
Claudine unhappy by scolding her. I like being dependent on
you and being a little frightened of a friend I love so much.

I want to tell you something else too; it's that I shan't come
back to Paris. You have entrusted me to the country I love, so
come and find me again here, keep me here, love me here. If
you have to leave me sometimes, because you have to or
because you want to, I will wait here faithfully and with no
mistrust. There is enough beauty and sadness here in Fresnois
for you to have no fear of boredom if I am with you all the
time. For I am more beautiful here, more loving, more sincere.

Whatever happens, come, because I can't go on any longer
without you. I love you, I love you; it's the first time I've
written it to you. Come! Remember that I have just been
waiting four whole long days, my dear husband, for you not
to be too young for me any more ...